THE MORNING GIFT

Published under licence by Brown Dog Books and
The Self-Publishing Partnership Ltd, 10b Greenway Farm, Bath Rd, Wick, nr.
Bath BS30 5RL

www.selfpublishingpartnership.co.uk

ISBN printed book: 978-1-83952-425-7
ISBN e-book: 978-1-83952-426-4

Cover design by Kevin Rylands
Internal design by Andrew Easton

Printed and bound in the UK

This book is printed on FSC certified paper

THE MORNING GIFT

The troubled quest of an
Anglo-Saxon princess

RUTH BURN

CONTENTS

INTRODUCTION

Osryth was brought up in Bamburgh, the home of the Northumbrian royal family. This novel describes her adventures in the year AD 675. During this eventful year she married Aethelred, who had recently become the king of Mercia. Several weeks later she undertook a challenging journey to Bardney to bury the last remains of her uncle, King Oswald of Northumbria. He had been killed in battle against the Mercians several decades earlier. There was a long history of warfare between Northumbria and Mercia.

AD 675 was not a straightforward year for the province of Mercia. King Wulfhere of Mercia waged an unsuccessful campaign against King Ecgfrith of Northumbria. On his return Wulfhere became ill and died. His younger brother Aethelred became king of Mercia. When Aethelred married Osryth, a sister of Ecgfrith, this must have come as an unwelcome surprise to many Mercians and Northumbrians.

Much of this novel is based on real people and events but inevitably it is a work of fiction. Details of that period are sketchy. In Anglo-Saxon times it was the custom for a bride to be given a gift the morning after the wedding. This then became her property. Aethelred gave Osryth a present of high value the day after their marriage. Much of the story turns around what happens to the gift over the course of a year. I have woven an account from the facts that I have gleaned about this independent and strong-willed princess and the era in which she lived.

I was inspired by the finding of the Staffordshire Hoard in 2009 to write this book. There have been many exhibitions of the items found in the trove since then. The vast array of jewelled remnants of battle, undisturbed in the ground for over 1,000 years, has intrigued many people. Some experts have dated the artefacts to about AD 675 with some of the items dating back as much as a couple of decades earlier.

This novel describes the journeys of Osryth. Her marriage to Aethelred, king of Mercia, involved travelling between the royal courts of Tamworth and Bamburgh. She visited the religious communities of Whitby where her mother and sister had settled and then Bardney Abbey where she eventually made her home. The central journey in this book concerns a mission by Osryth to bury the remains of her uncle, Oswald, a king of Northumbria. She wished to create a shrine for him in Bardney in Lincolnshire and wanted to honour his memory by taking her morning gift of gold, silver and jewellery, remnants of battles gone by, to his shrine.

Osryth was adventurous and full of stamina. She travelled widely both before and after her wedding to Aethelred. The historian Bede describes her journey to Bardney with the last remains of Oswald in his *Ecclesiastical History of the English People*. The name of Osryth appears on some of the charters actually signed by her husband Aethelred; this shows where she was and those she was with at certain times.

In this book the journey from Tamworth to Oswestry along Watling Street took Osryth past the spot where the Staffordshire Hoard was found near the crossroads of Ryknild Street and Watling Street. This novel describes how Osryth made a disastrous decision regarding her morning gift.

I have quoted excerpts of the ancient poem *Beowulf* at the beginning of each chapter in this book. I have been given permission to quote from the translation by Seamus Heaney. *Beowulf* has a similar theme to this book with its emphasis on travelling and treasure and it conveys a very real impression of those times

There are many journeys undertaken in this book; the central one relates to Osryth travelling to Bardney. Journeys by boat were popular in the Anglo-Saxon era. This book describes the contrasts between different methods of travel, the contrast in the landscape and culture of the different regions and the strains caused in the marriage between two people whose families have been at war.

Although this novel is a work of fiction it is based on people and events that actually existed. I have invented a connection between Osryth and the Staffordshire Hoard. It is unlikely that the actual source of the hoard will ever be definitively proved but it is quite possible that there is at least some connection particularly in view of the location and the dates.

PROLOGUE

'... Rusty helmets
all eaten away. Artfully wrought
armbands everywhere. How easily can treasure
buried in the ground, gold hidden
however skilfully, escape from any man!'
Lines 2762-6 *Beowulf* **(Seamus Heaney)**

A desolate spot. Three women stand at the edge of the
dark forest near the crossroads of the old Roman roads
of Watling Street and Ryknild Street. In the half-light of
early morning the heathland looks bleak.

One of the three figures leans down to the ground
and rakes out clumps of damp earth. The other two drag
a large linen bag from a cart and place it on the ground. A
horse waits patiently with bowed head. All three women
tuck up their long skirts and sleeves. They are totally
absorbed in their task. It has rained gently overnight
and the grass is damp. The smell of wild garlic hangs
heavy in the air. Clumps of soil are piled up around the
shallow hole and after a short interval the linen bag is
heaved into the dip in the ground. The newly dug earth
is gently placed on top of the mound and small heaps
of undergrowth and some decaying leaves are added.

11

Two large sticks are placed into the ground to mark the spot. The eldest of the three women takes off her amber necklace and places it on a branch of a tree. Far above them a magpie watches with steely eyes.

An omen of trouble to come?

PART 1
SPRING

CHAPTER 1
A VISIT TO WHITBY ABBEY

SIX WEEKS EARLIER
TUESDAY, EARLY APRIL AD 675.

'...the harp being struck
and the clear song of a skilled poet
telling with mastery of man's beginnings'
Lines 90-92 *Beowulf*

A small dog lay resting on the floor of the abbey in a pool of sunlight. It was curled up and appeared deep in slumber. Suddenly its ears flicked up. A distant rumble could be heard. 'Is that thunder or could it be the sound of horses' hooves? Not an invading army I trust,' said Eanfled to her daughter, her brow furrowed, the colour draining from her face.

'No, Mother. We are quite safe here in Whitby. We do not have enough possessions to warrant a raid. Maybe we have some unexpected visitors,' replied her daughter Aelfflaed. 'Didn't my sister Osryth send a message that she hoped to visit? It may well be her retinue that we hear.'

It was nearly Easter. Outside the abbey the weather was blustery. Clouds scudded along but the sun shone brightly and the sea sparkled far down below. The smell of salt and seaweed wafted up in the breeze.

The late afternoon sunlight streamed through a window casement in the abbey buildings. It cast a flickering trellis of light on the wooden panel opposite. Aelfflaed, a slim young woman in her early twenties, was at her writing desk trying out different coloured inks. Her mother Eanfled was seated nearby with her needlework. Each was dressed in a plain long tunic and simple headdress. Each wore a necklace that glinted in the sunlight.

The murmuring of the sea seemed louder than usual. Aelfflaed looked up. The rhythm of horses' hooves seemed closer. The sound stopped and she looked out of the window opening. Seagulls were darting hither and thither freewheeling in the strong breeze.

The horses must have been tethered further down the hill. Two figures could be seen climbing the last few steps. The windswept pair had a familiar air. As they approached Aelfflaed realised with a shock of delight that her sister Osryth was one of the two. Her tall upright frame and flowing fair hair were unmistakable. Aelfflaed roused her mother from her reverie. 'We must go and greet them,' she said.

They hurried to the entrance. Their visitors were gazing with interest at the haphazard but picturesque rectangle of wooden buildings surrounding a central cloister. In the near distance the outline of surrounding farms could be seen. Osryth's long tunic and cloak billowed around her. Her ornate brooch gleamed in a shaft of sunlight. Her companion was a tall, fair-haired young man with regular features. His clothes, although dusty, were made of fine cloth. When he spoke in greeting Aelfflaed suddenly recognised him. He was Aethelred, brother-in-law to both her much older step-sister and her half-brother. She had met him once before at the royal hall in Tamworth. He was not a relation by blood but linked to them by the marriages of his older siblings. She was surprised to see him. It was the first time he had visited Whitby.

'Greetings to you both. I know you sent word recently, Osryth, that you hoped to visit. But what a happy surprise. I was not expecting to see Aethelred too. I did not know that you were well acquainted,' Aelfflaed said as she ushered the couple in from outdoors. Both were glowing from their exercise and they took a seat in the scriptorium. She enquired after their retinue. Aethelred replied 'My men have found lodgings in the small settlement of Whitby down the hill.' Aelfflaed realised that he was a man of few words but direct and plain in his speech.

As the visitors entered the building the small dog sprang to attention and Eanfled stroked it gently.

'My dear Osryth, we were just wondering about you,' said her mother. 'How often my thoughts return to the court in Bamburgh. I cannot believe it is five years since your father died. We were so close and now here we are together again. And who is this with you? Your companion looks familiar – have I met him before?'

Osryth replied, 'I too think of those happy days – they seem so long ago – and now life has been kind to me again.' And then she added, 'This is Aethelred of Mercia. I have been staying at Tamworth with his sister; her children are our nephews and nieces. Have you not met Aethelred before?'

Eanfled looked puzzled. 'Aethelred must be the same age as your brother Ecgfrith. They lived together for a while in Mercia when they were boys.' Then she spoke directly to the young man, 'Do you remember? You must have been about nine years old – that is a long while ago. Do not be surprised if I did not recognise you.'

After a slight pause Aethelred replied, 'I remember Ecgfrith well. We had a big household. He lived with us for nearly two years, as I recall.'

Eanfled's eyes closed for a moment as she remembered the pain of giving up her own son to a hostile kingdom. To her it seemed like yesterday and the distress still felt raw. She shook her head to try to banish these memories. She said to her guests, 'Now to the present - you must have travelled for many days to reach here. I hope that the journey here from Tamworth was not too difficult.'

Osryth replied, 'We have had fair weather and Aethelred's men knew their way. How good it is to see you. You look the same as ever.' Then she added affectionately, 'Perhaps your hair is a shade lighter. But grey hair suits you. You look well. And you are still near the sea. You always said that since your days in Kent you could not imagine living far away from it. And this abbey reminds me so much of our home in Northumbria situated as it is on a clifftop; you must surely feel the same. Perhaps this does not look so much like a fortress.'

Her mother agreed with her. 'The fencing you see along the hillside is to protect us from the strong winds and to keep our livestock safe. Your father chose this spot well; there are many fields of good farming land and a busy fishing port down there.' As she spoke she pointed down to the inlet with its cluster of boats.

Osryth continued. 'I have missed you so much, you wouldn't believe. I wish that I had found an opportunity to visit you before. My brothers were not so keen on travelling such distances. They do not know what they have missed, the countryside here is so beautiful,' she said looking around her, adding, 'the stone church is so well situated on the brow of the hill. And the scriptorium here is right next to it. What views you must have. No wonder you spend much of your time here. You must show me round.' She looked around at the monastery buildings and outhouses. 'This must be a hive of activity. There are far more people both in the settlement down below and the community here on the hillside than I ever expected. I suppose everyone is kept busy; the bakehouse, the forge and the farms must require a lot of attention and oversight,' she exclaimed, and then she said reflectively, 'Later you must show me the grave of my father; it must give you great comfort it is so close by.'

'But I do often wish that the remains of my own father could rest in peace here too. I could tend his grave and place flowers there,' murmured Eanfled. 'Perhaps one day...' and her voice trailed away. Sometimes the past seemed more real to her than the present.

Vespers, late afternoon prayers, had already been said and it was not yet time for Compline, the evening service. As was the custom, a meal was to be served in the meantime. The visitors were hungry and thirsty and so Aelfflaed took her sister Osryth to the refectory to request that those in the kitchen make two more meals. A meal of vegetable broth, rye bread and goat's cheese was being prepared. The smell of the broth wafted through the kitchen and refectory. Under the watchful eyes of Abbess Hilda the abbey had become famous for its hospitality. Aelfflaed hoped that Osryth would feel welcome; the two sisters did not see each other as often as they would have liked.

Aelfflaed reflected how differently the lives of the two sisters had turned out. Each day was similar at the abbey. The days followed in a gentle rhythm one after another and the only difference seemed to be a change in the weather and the pattern of the different seasons. She was kept busy with daily chores and monastic duties. This life was really all that Aelfflaed had known. Her father Oswy had handed her over to Hilda many years previously as a thanksgiving for a success in battle. Occasionally she was wistful and thought about what her life would have been like if he had not done so. She may well have grown up in Bamburgh with the rest of her family. And maybe she would have had children herself one day. These thoughts flitted into her head from time to time. She tried to banish them. She was content with her lot, even more so after having been joined by her mother. She had heard that Osryth was restless at Bamburgh. Much had changed there in recent years since the death of their father. No wonder her sister liked to travel. Osryth must have been very determined to complete the long journey to Tamworth from Bamburgh and then travel on to Whitby; she would soon face the daunting prospect of returning back to her home from Whitby. Horseback was not comfortable for long periods. The roads were uneven and the deep potholes were hazardous. Wagons could overturn. Nevertheless Aelfflaed could understand what had driven her sister to make the journey. Her home in Bamburgh was no doubt now very different in the absence of both her parents.

Aelfflaed was surprised to see Aethelred. He had recently become king of Mercia after the illness and death of his brother, Wulfhere, who had until recently been fighting in Northumbria. Why was Aethelred not occupied with affairs of state? Was he here because he was curious to visit Whitby Abbey? Aelfflaed wondered. The abbey was well known. Delegates from far and wide had attended the church assembly, the synod, there eleven years previously. Despite the dreadful plague that preceded and followed it, a plague that had lasted for several years, the assembly had marked an important milestone in church practices and faith was not lost, if anything it was strengthened. The date of Easter was no longer in question. Perhaps word had eventually spread to Mercia about the growing renown of the abbey. She hoped that Aethelred came in peace and would respect their community. Time would tell.

Aelfflaed showed her sister around the refectory and kitchen greeting those who were preparing the meal. She said, 'You were right about a hive of activity, Osryth, there are many mouths to feed in this community. But visitors are always welcome.'

'I do hope so,' replied Osryth. 'It has been a long journey here.' Tempting smells of steaming vegetables pervaded the refectory and Osryth became conscious of pangs of hunger. She felt disconcerted. Despite her words of welcome Aelfflaed had looked surprised to see Aethelred and her mother had actually looked shocked. Osryth hoped that they would feel some warmth towards the newcomer. Osryth knew of the troubled history between Mercia and Northumbria. She was too young to remember the siege of Bamburgh but she knew of the tensions between the two kingdoms. Things had calmed down after the death of Aethelred's father but danger always simmered in the background. But Aethelred himself had not been part of these troubles.

He had not been brought up to expect that he would be a king. He would not have expected that his eldest brother Paeda would be killed nor that his elder brother Wulfhere would die of illness at a comparatively young age. Aethelred was the third son of Penda and had grown up hunting and pursuing other outdoor activities. Despite his upbringing, he was now of the same faith as themselves. Perhaps, she thought, the happy news they brought with them on this journey would change things for the better.

When the two sisters went to visit the kitchen their mother Eanfled was left alone with Aethelred. She said to him, 'I hope that you did not encounter any mishaps on your journey and that your horses remain well shod. We do have a forge here if needed and stables too if you wish to keep the horses comfortable and well fed with hay.'

'I will check tomorrow,' replied Aethelred.

Despite her polite words Eanfled was puzzled about the reason for Aethelred's visit. She felt apprehensive and looked wary. She had a sickening feeling in the pit of her stomach. There was a dawning realisation that Aethelred was the son of the late King Penda of Mercia. Penda had caused the Northumbrians, and her family in particular, endless misery. She could see a resemblance to his father in the set of his jaw. He looked as though he too would not easily be swayed from any course he chose to undertake. Why had Osryth befriended him? She thought back to the past. Eanfled knew only too well of Penda's fearsome reputation. He had been involved in many wars; many kings and princes from different parts of the country had fallen in battle because of him. He had been responsible for the brutal death of her brother-in-law, Oswald, thirty years previously. It was just as well that Oswy, her husband, had defeated Penda ten years later, she thought to herself. It had seemed that Penda had a particular contempt for Oswy. Her husband had done all he could to avoid warfare. Their son Ecgfrith had been placed as a young boy with the Mercian royal family in effect as a hostage. Eanfled herself had seemed to have very little say in what happened. Oswy had later handed over huge amounts of treasure to Penda to avert a battle. It was a great loss to their kingdom. A visit from the youngest son of Penda was disconcerting to say the least. Her husband might well be turning in his grave. She remembered the difficult history only too well.

More than two decades had passed since that time. Eanfled realised it was time for bygones to be bygones and that she should welcome this tall stranger. She felt troubled. Why had her husband Oswy encouraged the marriage alliances of the past between the royal families of Northumbria and Mercia? she thought to herself. There was no getting away now from a family connection. Were they forever to be entangled? Why had she not foreseen Aethelred and her daughter getting better acquainted? As these thoughts flitted through her mind Eanfled realised that she must have seemed distracted. She did not want to be discourteous. Eanfled enquired after Aethelred's sister.

'She is well,' she was assured. 'And so are her children who have filled the royal hall with laughter and merriment.' Aethelred hesitated; he added slowly that his reason for visiting at short notice was to ask for Osryth's hand in marriage. He was here to ask for the permission of her mother. 'I am sorry if my arrival here has come as a surprise to you. I thought that you had been sent a message that I was planning to visit. I am here to ask you for your consent for me to marry your daughter, Osryth.'

Eanfled, mother of Osryth, was taken aback. Despite his appearance the young man was so unlike Penda in his manner. She should have anticipated this turn of events. After all, Osryth was beautiful and a good match for anyone. She came from a good family. Her own lineage was impressive. He was a fortunate young man. She said to him. 'I thought that now I was sheltered from the world in this remote part of the country that no longer would my advice or consent be needed for anything important, and that my days would pass in tranquillity and without worry.'

'But this news is meant to be joyful and not a matter of concern for you.' Aethelred smiled. The smile transformed his face. Nevertheless Eanfled felt uneasy. Did he not know the family history? Aethelred added, 'And I am offering all the treasure that I possess in exchange for her hand in marriage.'

Eanfled replied, 'And what is that treasure? I do not want to sound mercenary but very few of the men in our families have a long life; either they are killed in battle or they are overcome by disease. Osryth will need some fortune of her own. If you die she should live in comfort. As indeed so should any children you may have. Please give your treasures to Osryth rather than to her family. Now I have no need of worldly goods, nor does Aelfflaed. My husband founded this abbey and has ensured that I am well looked after. At long last I know peace and serenity in my life.'

Aethelred smiled again. She did indeed look serene. The well-ordered life of the monastery and the fresh sea air suited her. Her grey hair was neatly tucked away and her habit was clean and fresh. He knew that despite their royal blood that both she and her daughter Aelfflaed would assist with the daily tasks. It was fortunate that she lived in a double monastery where the monks could do much of the outdoor work and tend to the animals. He had heard of Caedmon, their swineherd and stable hand. Caedmon not only looked after the animals but also wrote poetry and was known for his singing. Hilda the abbess had encouraged his talent. No wonder Northumbria was regarded as the centre for learning and culture.

Aethelred was aware that everything seemed much more rough and ready in Mercia. He reflected that at least their people knew where they stood. They were either in the category of royalty, a thegn, a ceorl or a slave. Everyone had their place. And Christianity was a relatively new religion in Mercia. It was longer established in the north of the country. It seemed to have blurred some of the usual boundaries. Aethelred looked at Eanfled's slight figure and still elegant hands. She no doubt concentrated on her fine needlework and her daughter Aelfflaed was becoming noted for her writing and illustration of texts. He had heard that she was also becoming learned in medical matters. Despite her young age her dexterity in surgical skills was known far and wide. She shared her knowledge of medicines and herbal remedies with the novices at Whitby.

'I am more than happy to have an alliance with the family of Osryth and now that I have met you I am even more aware of my good fortune. Of course Osryth will be free to do what she wishes with the morning gift. It will be a token of my gratitude for our marriage,' Aethelred said.

How could Eanfled resist such words? She relaxed slightly and said slowly, 'At least I hope that you marry Osryth out of affection rather than just in the hope of bringing together the great kingdoms of Mercia and Northumbria. That has already been attempted and not altogether with success.'

Aethelred smiled again. 'You need not doubt our affection for one another, which has grown over recent times and our sincere wish that our families should be united rather than be at war.'

At this point Osryth and Aelfflaed entered the room. Eanfled was saved from making any answer to the young man. The two sisters beckoned to their mother and their guest and they made their way to the refectory. It was a large square wooden building to the west of the monastery. Sturdy trestle tables were placed against the walls with long benches for seating. A fire smouldered in the middle of the room giving an appearance of warmth.

The elderly Abbess Hilda sat at the head of the table and looked at her guests with a kindly expression. Her eyes were watery; she had recently suffered from poor sight and hearing. She seemed older than her years. But she ran the abbey as calmly and efficiently as ever. She could not help but be surprised by her guests. She had heard about the hostility in the past between the royal families of Mercia and Northumbria. Sometimes life seemed stranger than fiction she thought as she met the young couple. This made her all the more determined to give a welcome. To mark the importance of the occasion of royal visitors, mead was served with the meal and a harpist played in the background. One of the monks was prevailed upon to entertain the guests with his verse. Hilda introduced him. 'This is Caedmon, of whom I am so proud. He is now one of the brethren. He still tends the cattle as he used to do but he now spends much of his time composing verse. Only recently has he felt able to sing to us. He had a dream that he could do this and we are now much blessed.' Caedmon stepped forward. He was a young man who had the fresh complexion and the rough hands of one who has spent much time outdoors. But he looked comfortable in his robes and had a quiet confidence about him.

After the introduction by Hilda Caedmon said quietly to the gathered community, 'I am honoured to sing in front of you all and in particular to our royal visitors. I do hope that they feel welcome and that I can do the verse some justice.'

Caedmon's words sounded like a hymn of worship. He sang in his own simple dialect and in the phrases he had composed himself. They were all encompassing and his words sounded genuine and heartfelt. He praised the maker of the world and the intricacy of the universe and the wonder of it. He sang accompanied by the harp. He had a resounding voice and Aethelred was spellbound by the words.

It did seem that the dramatic site of Whitby made one more receptive to this beautiful verse. Aethelred wondered what caused the special magic in this place. He very rarely came across poetry or informal worship of God in Mercia. He resolved to go more to the church in Lichfield when back in Mercia. He hoped that would have a similar uplifting effect; he was not convinced that it would. He found the words of this simple farmhand more telling than the addresses given by the learned bishops.

In her turn, Osryth sighed with relief that this modest looking monk sang in English rather than Latin. She whispered to Aethelred, 'Thank goodness we can understand him. I wonder how long his words will be remembered – perhaps for longer than just our generation.' She and Aethelred were neither as well read in Latin as those from the monastic community. At least they could both appreciate his words as well as the music. As she sat and ate the nourishing meal and drank some mead she pondered on her good fortune. She wanted to make the most of this. She experienced a warm glow of joy. However, at the back of her mind there was a slight presentiment. She shuddered slightly at the thought that her joy may be premature and that something may go wrong.

'The treasure that you mentioned that you will give to Osryth – what is its origin?' Eanfled asked Aethelred towards the latter part of the meal.

Aethelred looked uncomfortable. 'I received it after my brother Wulfhere passed from this life.'

'From where does it originate?' Eanfled said in a low voice, fearing the answer.

'I am not sure,' came the reply. 'My father died when I was quite young and it was something that my mother did not talk about. I only know that my father was determined that Mercia be the most successful kingdom and he did not flinch from fighting.'

'The Northumbrians do not need reminding of that,' Eanfled said. The three women had turned pale. Eanfled shivered. The battles between Mercia and Northumbria had been long and drawn out and had caused the death of Eanfled's brother-in-law, Oswald. Oswald was now venerated as a saint. How strange that Aethelred planned to marry the niece of his father's long-time enemy. At least since the death of Oswald, Penda had not been averse to the conversion of his offspring to Christianity; he may well have thought it to be politically expedient but it did give some hope for the future.

Aethelred looked uneasy. 'As you rightly say it will provide her with a comfortable fortune if I have the misfortune to die early.'

It was difficult to feel angry with this young man who could only have been a small boy when his own father died and who was not even born when the Battle of Maserfield took place. But it suddenly felt cold in the early evening air as they strolled around the abbey grounds after their meal and they all shivered.

They changed the subject and talked about the forthcoming wedding. 'Where should it be?' asked Aelfflaed. They looked around at the beautiful setting, the abbey standing majestically on a hill, the sea down below. It would be difficult to think of a better place.

'We have already discussed this,' said Osryth. 'It will be in Aethelred's royal hall at Tamworth. Bishop Winfrith has agreed to give the blessing at the end of the ceremony; he is an old friend of Aethelred's family in Mercia. He was sorry to miss the coronation of Aethelred after the sad illness and death of his brother Wulfhere. The wedding will be held in a month's time on the fifteenth of May; the weather should be more clement and the celebrations can last for days. You are most welcome to attend.'

Her mother was taken aback that all the details had been sorted out before any discussion. 'But what about my cousin Hilda?' said Eanfled. 'She will not be well enough to travel that distance. She will be disappointed not to attend.'

Osryth said flatly, 'Well I am afraid that it has all been sorted out and really it will only be close family who will attend on our side. We do not want to wait too long to get married. Wherever the wedding is held it would be inconvenient for some. Aethelred is very keen that the ceremony should be in Mercia. His sister and her family live in Peterborough. Tamworth is a good halfway point.' There was no chance of further debate. Eanfled fell silent.

It was time for Compline and they all repaired to the chapel. The chants of the monks were comforting to all and the prayers were said with added meaning. Eanfled felt that she should be glad. However, her feeling of discomfort had not left her and Aelfflaed looked troubled. They would talk with Osryth next morning. There would be plenty of time for that.

After the service Hilda beckoned to one of the monks. She said to him, 'Please show Aethelred to his accommodation and see that he has everything he needs. It would be worth taking at least one spare candle with you.' So both carried a candle that they took from the altar, each of them cupping their hands over the small flickering flame to ensure that it was not blown out by the wind. The face of the elderly monk was cast into strange shadows by the varying light. He guided Aethelred to one of the rooms set aside for guests and put a jug of water on the side.

Aethelred had been shown to a small rectangular stone building near the edge of the hillside in a line of similar buildings. 'These are the guest rooms at the north of the abbey. The large stone building that you see slightly set apart is the forge. The women have accommodation to the south of the abbey nearer the refectory. Their rooms are all similar. We can show you round properly tomorrow when it is light.' Aethelred looked around at his accommodation with curiosity. It was divided into two rooms by a thin partition. One room was a living area with a table and bench. Part of a loaf of bread and a small portion of butter were placed on the table. A candle flickered not far from a narrow window opening. With the light of that candle Aethelred could see his bedroom. There was a wooden-framed bed with a straw mattress that was covered by woollen blankets. A bolster served as a pillow. Aethelred was impressed. His guide saw him looking around and said, 'We are fortunate to live in comfortable conditions. I am glad that we can offer you one of these guest rooms. I hope

that you have a good night's sleep and wake refreshed.'
And with that the monk glided away with his lantern,
a slightly ghostly figure in his long robes disappearing
into the ever-darkening dusk. Aethelred called out after
him, thanking him for his trouble. There was no answer
and his voice seemed to float away in the wind.

Aethelred looked up and saw vast constellations of
stars dotted around in the darkening sky. As always
the night sky put everything else into perspective with
its vastness and with the sight of so many far distant
glimmers of light. The near silence was comforting;
at night-time the raucous cries of the seagulls were
quietened. There was no noise from the monastery. The
gentle rustle of the wind and the lapping of the waves on
the shore were the only sounds. He recalled the words
sang by Caedmon. He was impressed with Whitby and
very glad of a welcome. He knew that there would be
many challenges associated with a marriage to Osryth;
he was conscious that the history between the two
royal families that stretched back a long way had been
very troubled. His conviction was firm nevertheless.
Marrying Osryth was the only future he could imagine
for himself. He was thirty and a good age for marriage.
Osryth herself was almost ten years younger. He loved to
be in her company and he hoped that one day they would
have a family together. Young children running around
would certainly brighten up the hall in Tamworth. And,
as he reflected, surely Osryth's brother Ecgfrith would

not have encouraged his sister to visit Tamworth if he had not been keen to foster good relations. At least, Aethelred thought to himself, he had got over the first hurdle. There had been some reticence but no sign of antagonism from the family of Osryth here in Whitby. He was tired after his long journey and pleased to rest. He soon fell into a deep and untroubled sleep.

Silence was observed by the three women after Compline as was the custom. It was hard not to ask more questions but this could be done the next day. All three retired to their rooms. The beds were comfortable but sleep when it did come was fitful and fleeting. Eanfled took some time to fall asleep and then had recurrent nightmares of Bamburgh in flames and the wind driving the flames back. She woke with a start and lay awake reliving the past during the early hours. When she eventually fell back to sleep she tossed and turned; when she woke up she felt as though she had hardly slept at all. Aelfflaed had a more settled night but was also wide awake before daybreak. This was not unusual. The early morning was a good time for reflection and prayer as was the custom in the religious community. And sometimes too for study.

Osryth herself was excited about the prospect of her new life. In Bamburgh in recent years she had felt very separate from most of her family. Now she had found a new happiness and a fresh purpose in life. She knew Aethelred to be steady both in his affection and his intention to marry her. Despite this she could not help but wonder about the proposed morning gift. She, like her mother, was very curious about its origin. It would be difficult to speculate about the gift without actually seeing exactly what it was. Osryth wondered whether her plans for marriage would actually materialise into a pleasant reality or just vanish into thin air. Sometimes it seemed like a fantastical dream and any moment she felt that she might wake up.

Early next morning before breakfast the mother and daughters sat in the refectory at one of the tables. It was a most unusual family reunion. 'And are you content now, Osryth?' Eanfled asked. Really there was no need to put that question. Osryth looked happier than her mother had ever seen her.

'I do just have one reservation,' she replied and her face clouded over.

'And what is that?' said Aelfflaed and her mother in unison. They looked at one another. They had grown to be quite similar not only in their appearance but also in their manner in this restricted community.

The reply came slowly and hesitantly. 'I am very uncomfortable about the marriage gift, the morning gift that is planned. Aethelred does not really know that much about the history of our families and it is probably better that way. I am sure he means well. But do you remember all those years ago when we were planning to take what was left of Oswald's body from Oswestry and bury his mortal remains in the monastery of Bardney in Lincolnshire along with some treasure?'

'Was that the treasure your father gave to Penda in the vain hope of achieving peace? That was shortly before the last battle Penda fought. I do not think that Oswy was happy about giving away the treasure to Penda. It is the last thing your father would have wanted but at least he did try to avert war,' Eanfled said slowly to her two daughters. 'I married Oswy after his brother had been killed but I know how close they both were, particularly after growing up together on the small island of Iona. Oswy was devastated by the brutal murder of his brother at the battle of Maserfield. He could not understand why his brother's body had been hacked to pieces. He later gave many hides of land to Bardney in Lincolnshire for a monastery to be founded and for the purpose of honouring Oswald.'

'Do you think it would still be possible to take Oswald's remains to Bardney?' her elder daughter Osryth asked.

'That would be my greatest wish,' said Eanfled. 'Perhaps we could still take both Oswald's remains and some treasure. Perhaps this offering by the son of his old enemy is a sign that all things turn out for the best. And then my husband can sleep in peace in his grave here and we will be giving due honour to his brother. After all it was Oswy's wish that the religious community in Bardney be honoured in this way.'

'Do you think that you can write to the monks in Bardney to prepare them for this?' Aelfflaed asked her mother. 'Then if we attend the wedding in Tamworth we can assist on our return home here.'

Osryth said quickly, 'I can undertake this on my own. I do not want to draw you into this plan. Heaven only knows what may happen as a result of my enterprise. I had better not tell Aethelred about my plans for the treasure which he plans to give me. I would not be able to find the right words. But I will tell him that I want to fulfil my father's long-held wish to bury what remains of Oswald's body in Bardney. It will become a shrine no less than that of Lindisfarne and Durham. Aethelred will surely understand the importance of this to me before I settle down as his wife.'

Her mother questioned, 'Are you sure that you are doing the right thing? Had you better not tell him about your plans for the morning gift? Do you want to keep secrets from your husband even at this early stage of your marriage? Do think carefully about this. Such secrets never seem to end happily.'

Osryth replied, 'But what would be gained by telling him? It would only give him an opportunity to disapprove of such a thing. I cannot believe he would allow it and yet the treasure by rights will become mine and my honouring Oswald and Bardney with the treasure surely would make good the horrors of the past.'

But Osryth did inwardly wonder about the wisdom of the plan. The mission may right the wrongs of the past but would she ever forget the troubled family history? It would be good if everything could begin afresh.

CHAPTER 2
BETROTHAL

'Over the waves, with the wind behind her
and foam at her neck, she flew like a bird
until her curved prow had covered the distance'
Lines 217-219 Beowulf

Later that morning sunshine streamed through the casement window facing east. The wind had died down and the abbey was quiet. Eanfled had resolved to agree to the marriage of her daughter with the Mercian king. Despite her qualms she realised that it may well herald a new era. An end might be put to the many wars between the Mercian and Northumbrian kingdoms if the young couple were fortunate enough to have a family. Aethelred had already shown her the engagement ring he hoped to bestow on Osryth. 'It belonged to my mother,' he said with pride. She was moved by his attachment to the memory of his mother. Eanfled had met her once in the distant past. She remembered her with some affection and also gratitude; she had been kind to her eldest son Ecgfrith, who had been cast into the Mercian royal family, into the unknown, at a young age. Eanfled gave a brief glance at the ring that he proposed to bestow upon Osryth. It was a delicate and intricate gold ring.

And so at short notice, but according to custom, Eanfled arranged a betrothal ceremony. She asked the Abbess Hilda to preside.

The service had been announced at morning prayers. Figures flocked from all directions. The thegns who had accompanied the young couple climbed the steep steps to pay their respects. The lay members of the community lined the pathways that led from the monastery to the grey stone church. All were curious to see the young couple. Word had spread that they were from royal families who had long been at war with each other. Maybe this would herald a new beginning. Aethelred sat with Osryth and watched the monks and nuns flow into the building, the monks processing to one side of the church and the nuns to the other.

'Well, we are certainly creating a stir,' Osryth whispered to Aethelred. He was pleased at the reaction to the news. This was the happiest he had felt for a long while. The church was full. There was not room for all of the congregation and a good number stood at the back. They all craned forward for a better look of the young couple. This was the highlight of their week, almost as good as an actual wedding. Because Eanfled and Aelfflaed lived in Whitby in the abbey their background was taken for granted. They were treated as part of the wider family in the monastic community. But it was a rare treat to have visiting royalty. If the wedding was not going to be held here as they had heard, then they would make the most of this engagement ceremony.

Hilda beckoned the young couple forward. Both walked forward to the front of the church without hesitation. Osryth was still weary after her travels but she was pleased that this moment had arrived. Prayers were said. Later during the course of the service Aethelred and Osryth came further forward to the altar and he knelt in front of her offering the ring. She accepted it gracefully. Both wondered what the other was thinking. Their eyes met briefly. Osryth tried not to smile. It was a moment of relief that all had gone smoothly this far.

Following the betrothal ceremony the abbess said a short prayer for their future happiness. She wrapped an embroidered white linen cloth around both their hands. 'Nothing can separate us now,' whispered Osryth under her breath. As she spoke, sparrows darted around the rafters above them and Eanfled was reminded of how her father used to relate a sparrow flying in and through the warmth of a mead hall and then disappearing into the cold night as a metaphor for life itself. So true and even more poignant in troubled times, she thought. And she hoped that this latest development in the family history would make up for the troubles of times past and that it would be a source of happiness. The young couple would certainly need her prayers, she thought to herself.

The Abbess Hilda was pleased to have a part in the ceremony of betrothal. She knew that she would not be well enough to undertake the long journey to Tamworth for the wedding in May. Her health was declining and she easily tired. Even the rigorous routine of the abbey was almost too much for her. But she was delighted to have a small part in the future plans of the young couple; after all, she was related to Osryth and she looked forward to the day when Eanfled and Aelfflaed would take over the duties of abbess.

'I feel so honoured and blessed to carry out this ceremony. I only hope that everything turns out for the best and that nothing comes to spoil the joy of the young couple,' Hilda said to Eanfled after the ceremony. Her cousin only nodded. Eanfled's eyes were welling with tears; she felt a strange mix of happiness and foreboding at the thought of her daughter's marriage.

After the ceremony Osryth and Aethelred looked forward to their next adventure. 'I will introduce you to my brother Ecgfrith in Bamburgh. I am sure that he will be happy for this union to go ahead and he will be a good ally if all goes well. I had forgotten until my mother reminded me that you had lived together for a while when you were younger,' said Osryth to Aethelred.

They knew there were more hurdles to overcome. Osryth's brother Ecgfrith had been the king of Northumbria since the death of his father, Oswy, five years previously. It was important to be on good terms with him. Ecgfrith's own first marriage had been troubled and not helped by his religious advisers. It was important that he gave his blessing to their marriage. And

Osryth liked his new wife, Eormenberg. She had been warm and pleasant to Osryth when she was mourning the death of her father and the loss of her mother. Five years previously Osryth's father, Oswy, had died after a short illness. After this her mother had left for Whitby. Osryth had felt very alone in Bamburgh despite the company of her two brothers. Her brother Ecgfrith's first wife, Etheldreda, despite her religious fervour, had been wrapped up in her own problems. Osryth had not shed any tears when she left for a religious life in the Fens. Etheldreda had looked happy to leave. But Eormenberg was different. She was even then a favourite of Ecgfrith and a warm personality.

There would be very many mixed emotions for Osryth on her return to Bamburgh, the home of her childhood. She hoped that any tensions would evaporate when she introduced Aethelred. Osryth knew of several places to visit along the route to Bamburgh. She looked forward to this. Nevertheless there was some apprehension mingled with her optimism.

As Eanfled said farewell to her elder daughter and Aethelred, she promised to make and embroider a wedding gown for her daughter. 'I will find the finest material and make a dress for you,' she declared. 'Only the best will be good enough.' She would bring this to Tamworth in May. It would be embroidered in Osryth's favourite colours of blue and gold. This would certainly occupy Eanfled for the next few weeks. There would be no time for worrying about what the future held for her daughter. They would need to transport this dress in a cart that would be specially decorated for that purpose. There would be all the practical matters to sort out including plans for their journey and who would accompany them, and whether or not Hilda was well enough to look after the abbey at Whitby on her own.

Aethelred and Osryth set off from Whitby later that morning full of anticipation. They carried a letter of introduction to an old friend of Hilda's at the monastery at Hartlepool and another letter for the Abbot of Wearmouth. They would not notice the long journey to Bamburgh with their minds so occupied. This was an opportunity for Osryth to show Aethelred what remained of the religious community of Hartlepool where her sister Aelfflaed had first been placed with Hilda as a small child. She then planned to visit the thriving new monastery in Monkwearmouth further along the route. The young couple felt refreshed after their welcome at Whitby and they were relieved that the weather was good.

Osryth was looking forward to taking Aethelred at long last to her family home in Bamburgh with its spacious and ornate feasting hall and the homely wooden church on the headland. He had never visited that part of Northumbria before. 'It is a dramatic part of the world. I think you will be impressed with Bamburgh,' declared Osryth. 'And I will make sure that you are made to feel welcome there.'

The holy island of Lindisfarne was not too far away. She knew that both Aelfflaed and Hilda would be pleased if the young couple met Cuthbert, who was the prior there. He was a genial and kindly soul from a good family who had started life as a shepherd and then became a monk after experiencing a vision that had coincided with the death of Aidan, a holy man of Lindisfarne.

Horseback had been up to now the mode of transport but travelling by boat up the eastern coast was a possibility and the wind was fair. So a large boat was chosen down in the sheltered harbour and the young couple chose six thegns to man the oars and a young farm girl to accompany Osryth. She was a practical, cheerful girl looking forward to new adventures in her life. Living on one of the local farms had made her strong and resourceful, qualities that would be important on journeys such as the ones they were planning to undertake. She would be a good companion for Osryth. The vessel was captained by a boatman who was used to the unpredictable currents along the coast. The remainder of their retinue would travel up the coastline on horseback and meet them at Bamburgh. Their own horses could rest in the farm stables at Whitby until their return.

They were waved off from the small harbour in the late morning. With a fair wind they should arrive at Hartlepool by dusk. Osryth had never felt so happy. The fresh breeze, the sunshine and the feeling of adventure kept both her and Aethelred in good spirits.

The young farm girl, Anna, who was aged only just sixteen years, was happy to talk to anyone who cared to listen; the novelty of the situation had a very positive effect on her. She commented on the varying coastline, small inlets with a few settlements and boats tied up and then, further along, long sweeping beaches with waves lapping gently along the shore; later they passed even more dramatic coastline with seabirds, gulls and guillemots darting along between the tufts of grass on dramatic cliff faces. The sky remained a clear blue. The first day passed in a sort of dream. The vessel they were in was far more comfortable in the good weather than horseback. They were regaled with stories of seafaring from the fisherman who was in charge of the boat. A smile was never far from his face. He was fond of riddles. Did he spend all his spare time working out the next riddle? wondered Osryth. He would test their quickness and knowledge of language and he was not at all intimidated by the status of his passengers. He was amused that Anna and the thegns sometimes came up with the answer to his riddles before the bemused royal couple. 'Right then,' he cried, 'what do you think I am referring to when I say, "Various shades of yellow and white, I emerge from a distant place at start of night, you see my face as clear as day, though you are so far away." I will let you think a while.' And he smiled at their puzzled faces. When eventually the answer 'moon' was given he gave a cheer. 'And have a guess at this one,' he added. 'Can you work it out? "I love the dark, damp ground. My home is my castle and I leave a trail of gleaming silver before hiding away." What do you think I am referring to?' And he prompted them with some clues. 'Yes, of course, the answer is a snail.'

And then he asked them to guess the name of his boat.

'Is it "Sea Dazzle" or "Spin Drift"?' asked Aethelred after a moment's thought. And Osryth made some other suggestions. They asked the boatman who was closer to the answer. 'Well I have not yet named it, if you must know,' said the boatman smiling broadly. 'They are all good suggestions. But the first name "Sea Dazzle" sounds very appropriate and I can tell people that my boat has been named by royalty – they will be very impressed I should think.' And so the time passed pleasantly.

They were never far away from the coastline. They saw the fishing nets and lines heaped neatly to one side of the boat. Osryth hoped that the boatman could catch some fish when they arrived in the harbour at Hartlepool. That would make a good offering and be a good way to thank their hosts for their hospitality.

All those on the boat were grateful for the gentle gusts of wind and the favourable currents hastening them along. A small sail had been raised. The thegns' rowing had a gentle but almost hypnotic rhythm. The anchor was dropped eventually at twilight in the inlet of Hartlepool. The monastery buildings were immediately evident. They alighted from the boat feeling a little dizzy from the day's sailing. 'It is almost as if I am intoxicated,' said Osryth. 'I feel giddy and light-headed. It must be the sway of the boat that I still feel. But how good it is to arrive here.' One of the thegns had preceded them and given notice of their arrival. Unexpectedly a welcome party stood at the water's edge. Candles were dotted around in the rapidly darkening dusk giving an impression of a myriad of stars.

All thoughts of the treasure offered by Aethelred and its strange origin were forgotten. The joy of travelling was too immediate for any such problems to dissipate Osryth's joyful mood. As she walked through the pointed arch built into the sea wall she looked up at the monastery buildings. Torches had been lit along the path to the monastery; they brightened up the dusk and gave a clear picture of the layout of the settlement. There were several small clusters of wooden outbuildings along the curved headland. Some of the structures looked uninhabited and others had begun to decay. Ivy was growing up the side of a few of the decaying buildings and was threatening to take over. Tangled dark strands grew up as far up as the thatched roofs which were now patched with green. The ivy looked sinister in the shadows cast by the lit torches. A few of the small, square wooden buildings looked well-tended and their gardens were neat and colourful. A long cloistered gallery led to a cemetery on the east side. There were also gravestones on the west side of the building. They must be for the lay people, Osryth thought to herself, and the graves to the east would be for those from the monastic community. The sun rose in the east. The altar to the east of the church was such an integral part of their faith; this was reflected by the ordering of the graves.

Osryth looked around with interest. She loved the coastline as much as her mother and thought rather wistfully of Tamworth which would be her home after marrying Aethelred. The royal hall of Tamworth could not be further away from the sea. She knew from her recent visit that it was well placed near the meeting point of two rivers; she would not be far away from water even in Mercia and she knew, whether it was for washing or drinking, how important that was for everyday life. However, the countryside around Tamworth was pleasant but in no way dramatic. She hoped that she would not feel too homesick.

Later that evening they were shown to the guest house attached to the old monastery. The evening was getting cool and they sat inside on a bench talking with an elderly lady who had served in the Abbey with Hilda. She said that she had known Hilda's mother who had often related to her a dream that Hilda was given a necklace that shone so brightly that it illuminated the whole world. She now tended the graves of both Hilda's mother and sister; every time she saw their names on the memorial slabs she was reminded of them.

Osryth replied, 'That dream of Hilda's mother is becoming a reality. Hilda is indeed a light that shines far and wide.'

The nun nodded in reply and then said, 'Please tell Hilda that we clear the headstones of lichen. The yellow and white wild flowers called "bright eye" grow in profusion here. You may be interested, their Latin name means harmony, a good partnership and happy dreams. Hopefully this is a happy sign for you at this particular time. And I always think that Hilda would be pleased that we have such an abundance of this plant. The name seems so apt; they are such a splash of colour when they flower.' The two women went outside to look down at the ground but by now it was difficult to distinguish anything in the gathering gloom of night. She added, 'Last year too we planted yellow primroses and now they look so colourful. You will see them in the morning. These flowers will ensure that when we are no longer here that there is some brightness on the ground for people to see and then perhaps it will remind them of us. Hilda should be pleased that her mother and sister lie in such a beautiful spot and that there is a worthy memorial to them both.'

'I am sure that is so,' replied Osryth.

The nun was anxious to talk and went on. 'We in this community here are all getting old now; there are not many of us left and we have to plan for the future. My joints are now getting stiff and I am slow to move – it is fortunate that the other members of the community are so kind to me.'

'It is very good of you to take the trouble to show me around. You must point out the graves,' said Osryth. 'Hilda will be so pleased to hear about your efforts. And I love the name of the flowers. I will take it as a happy omen. I will relate all this to her on my return.'

And so the time passed in reminiscence and quiet reflection. The thegns and Aethelred had retired to their quarters and Osryth and her serving girl Anna at last could relax. Anna had the smallest anteroom and Osryth quite a spacious guest room next door. Anna chatted about the journey with the excitement of youth. 'I have never travelled by boat before. I did not know it was such a relaxing and exciting way to journey.'

And Osryth smiled and replied, 'Well, we were very fortunate with the weather and the wind blowing in the right direction. The real test will be what you think after a bad spell of weather.'

Anna agreed. The guest beds provided by the monastery were lined with straw topped by woollen blankets and although the blankets were made of rough wool they both slept well and arose early. Aethelred and his men were already up and dressed. There was much to do. After a good meal of malt bread and cheese they all returned to the harbour where the boat was waiting. Some fish had been caught in the very early morning by the boatman and delivered as a gift to their hosts for their hospitality.

And again there was a fair wind as they made their way to Wearmouth to see the monastery built on land given by Osryth's brother, Ecgfrith. Word had spread around about the beautiful stained glass from Gaul that Benedict Biscop, the prior, had introduced there. They had also heard of the vast library of books collected by him. He had travelled abroad on a few occasions with Wilfred, a priest well known to them both who was now bishop of all Northumbria. Wilfred was a familiar face at Bamburgh. Benedict Biscop himself was universally popular with all he met whatever their religious sympathies. He had been a thegn at Oswy's court and had worked in Canterbury for a while. He was an accomplished, well-travelled priest with a far-reaching outlook. He was determined to make his church in Wearmouth a centre of culture and learning. He wanted his church community in the north east of the country to be remembered as a golden age; he would not rest until he accomplished this aim.

By contrast, Benedict's erstwhile travelling companion Wilfred could be a controversial figure. He was regarded with some suspicion by Hilda the abbess. It was unusual for her to dislike anyone. Hilda was unimpressed by the pomp and ceremony that Wilfred seemed to enjoy. Hilda had preferred the Celtic customs of Aidan. She knew her cousin Eanfled supported Wilfred: in Kent Eanfled had been influenced by the priest Paulinus who was also very much of the Roman persuasion. Eanfled, unlike

Hilda, had supported Wilfred a decade earlier when he had advocated the Roman practice rather than the Celtic viewpoint at the assembly in Whitby. And the Roman view had prevailed much to the consternation of some.

There was another bone of contention within the wider family. Wilfred had managed to antagonise Ecgfrith, now king of Northumbria, by siding with his first wife Etheldreda. He had encouraged her to be distant to her husband when Ecgfrith himself had been desperate for an heir. Some wondered exactly what Wilfred's motivation had been. Was it due to his religion, or was it really because he was fond of Etheldreda himself, or maybe it was because he was aware that Ecgfrith was having an affair with Eormenberg who Ecgfrith eventually married? Osryth tried to explain the complicated situation to Aethelred.

'Not that Ecgfrith and his first wife were ever particularly fond of each other anyway,' added Osryth. 'It really was just a marriage of convenience.'

'What complicated webs we all weave,' said Aethelred to Osryth. She could not help but agree with him. And Aethelred said, smiling at her, 'Well, at least we do not need to worry about our forthcoming marriage. At least we chose this path ourselves and no one forced us into it. I can see that that would not be a good start.'

They were both pleased that Benedict Biscop himself was a cultured, even-tempered man who took great pleasure in his library and works of art and tapestries and was delighted to show the young couple around. 'I hope that you take as much pleasure in viewing this new church and what it contains as I do showing you around,' he said to them.

The visit to the newly built church at Monkwearmouth was a short visit and they were shown their separate accommodation in the settlement. Close by the settlement was a herb garden which sloped down the grounds to the river. A pungent mix of fragrances filled the air, the aroma of lemon balm, lavender and basil to name just a few. Osryth and Aethelred breathed in the heady scent and they were pleased that the spring had been so warm and this area so sheltered.

The gardener and his wife who looked after guest rooms nearby were holding the hand of a bright-eyed young boy aged about three years. They said proudly to their guests, 'Our greatest hope is that in a few years our young son will be educated in the monastery; he shows great promise already. He has been given the name of Tiberius Bede by the monks. We are hoping that before long that the monks will take him under their wing. He is bright even at his young age and has learnt the names of all these different herbs and can tell you what medicines they can make.' Osryth and Aethelred smiled at the young boy; they hoped that one day that they would be equally proud of their own offspring.

Next morning, they looked around the church buildings again. Aethelred felt a little envious of the surroundings as he looked around the library and admired the stained glass. Benedict Biscop was very proud of his innovations. He was a tall, thin man with black hair and aquiline features. Nothing seemed to escape his notice. He had been determined to bring to England the best aspects of church architecture and culture that he had experienced on his many visits abroad. He employed skilled craftsmen from Gaul. He was more pleased than he could express that the young couple showed an interest. Prior to his clerical life he had served at Oswy's court. He was well acquainted with what had been going on at the court in Bamburgh for several years. He was pleased that Osryth would soon be married. He had heard that in recent years she had been quite lonely in the royal hall of Northumbria. Aethelred seemed a sensible man and hopefully there would be an end to the perpetual wars that had blighted the last three decades.

In the grey stone church there was a kaleidoscope of colours. The construction of the church had been completed the previous year. The stained glass and the rich colours of the wall hangings brightened up the interior. The young couple were told about the journeys required to transport the books and the stained glass from France. More than one trip had been made to acquire them. Several boats had been used. Benedict said, 'We should look to other countries, you know, if we can learn from them. It is no good being too proud and thinking that we always know best. It is only by appreciating the qualities in others wherever they come from that we can improve our own situation.'

The books were stacked high on the shelves in the library. They were leather-bound and the illuminated manuscript could only have been the result of many years' work. A picture of Aelfflaed working hard in the scriptorium suddenly flashed through Osryth's mind. 'How my sister would love to see all that you have here. She is also very talented at illustrating manuscripts. She would be so interested to see these.' The prior merely nodded his head and Osryth continued, 'I cannot believe the number of quill pens and assorted dyes for inks that must have been used to make these. It is almost too much to take in at first glance.'

Benedict Biscop said reflectively, 'Well, they were brought here for a reason. We do hope that this will attract the brightest minds and different talents here. If we make a success of this community we may well open yet another monastery on the other side of the river in a few years to carry on the good work.'

Osryth stared with wonder at the beautiful paintings hanging on the wall and the tapestries with gold thread that glimmered in the sunlight.

With a little disquiet Aethelred thought of Mercia. Nowhere there could compare with this, he thought uncomfortably. And for the first time he wondered whether Osryth would be happy in her new life with him. She had been so happy at Tamworth on a brief holiday with him in the company of their nephews and nieces. But her life would change so drastically once she was married. His Mercian nobles may find it difficult to accept a Northumbrian as the wife of their king. Equally, despite his welcome at Whitby he was not so naive as to think that that the family of Osryth would accept him without any qualms. The initial expression on Eanfled's face and even Aelfflaed's puzzled look on first meeting him was the proof of that. And Osryth herself had seemed a little reserved with him of late. Was she hiding something from him? Perhaps it was just his imagination, he told himself, trying to banish these uncomfortable thoughts. After all, it was apparent that she was enjoying the journey to her brother Ecgfrith's home. And it was good that she wanted them both to meet again.

And so as they embarked on the boat once again he asked her, 'Is anything amiss?'

She was surprised by the question. It was not like Aethelred to be unsure of himself. She looked so well and happy that the question seemed redundant and when she answered in the negative he knew he should have felt content. 'I am enjoying the journey more than I ever could have imagined,' she replied. And she touched his arm affectionately. But doubts continued to cloud his mind.

For some reason, and completely unexpectedly, Osryth recalled distant memories of her oldest half-brother, Alchfrid. She had been very conscious of his absence when she had stayed at Tamworth a few weeks earlier. His wife Cyneberga, Aethelred's sister, did not know what had happened to her husband. His children only had very distant memories of him. Alchfrid had disappeared shortly after attending the Synod of Whitby a decade previously. Cyneberga said there were rumours he had fled from his father Oswy after a disagreement and gone to a small monastery in Bewcastle in a remote area of Rheged. Either that or he may have died of the Plague that had ravaged the population at that time. A small church dedicated to Cuthbert had recently been constructed at Bewcastle. After the disappearance of her husband, Cyneberga herself had not felt safe at the Northumbrian court and had left it for the comparative safety of Mercia, being concerned about the protection of her own family. It seemed such a shame, Osryth thought, that there had been no word from him for so many years and she wondered if he was still alive. She was strongly of the opinion that if he had indeed died her eldest brother should have a memorial.

'Aethelred, I think that when we see Ecgfrith I will ask him his advice. Those Gaulish workmen in Wearmouth are so skilled. Do you think that Ecgfrith should ask them to create a cross to commemorate the life of my eldest half-brother, Alchfrid? You must remember him as well as I do, although I know that it is over ten years since anyone has seen him. How dreadful it must be for your sister to lose her husband like that.'

'I was not that well acquainted with Alchfrid, who spent most of his time in Northumbria. However, your idea is a good one. Those workmen are indeed so clever. I have not seen their like locally,' replied Aethelred.

The weather was greying over. The waves were edged with foam and sweeping along with ever greater force. However, the wind was still in the right direction and so the sail stayed up and the rowers took a rest every so often from their rowing. The provision of cold meat and bread was very welcome. Flagons of water and small casks of beer were stored under the seat and a box of apples from last year's harvest was tucked to one side of the boat.

It was dusk when they arrived at Bamburgh. They put the anchor down in an inlet close to an arch in the sea wall. Aethelred looked up with interest. The royal hall on the headland was well placed. Granite on volcanic rock looking down on the headland and the sea. No wonder his father had found it impenetrable and Wulfhere had not succeeded in his wars against Northumbria.

It looked as though visitors were an everyday occurrence. A number of boats were anchored in the harbour, bobbing up and down in the gentle swell. None quite so impressive as their own with its elaborate prow. But so many styles must indicate some visitors from far away. That in itself was reassuring. Those who lived there must be very hospitable. Nevertheless

Aethelred was a little nervous about meeting Ecgfrith. It was unlikely that Ecgfrith could forget that twenty years ago he had been offered in effect as a hostage to the Kingdom of Mercia and had been cared for in Tamworth by Aethelred's mother. Now he was much older, Aethelred realised that this arrangement may have been made by his father Penda to safeguard his own large family from attack. Aethelred recalled with disturbing clarity that Ecgfrith had often looked miserable; as a ten-year-old he had largely been ignored by Aethelred's older brothers and even though his sisters and mother had tried to be kind, Ecgfrith was evidently homesick for his own family. Aethelred himself had never disliked him but they did not have a lot in common. Ecgfrith had never wanted to join Aethelred on his hunting expeditions or his outdoor pursuits. What memories did Ecgfrith himself carry of this period of his childhood? Aethelred wondered.

Aethelred had an additional concern; he could not forget that his elder brother Wulfhere had waged a war against Ecgfrith as recently as a year previously. This was not the most auspicious background for an introduction to the family of his betrothed. He knew that Wulfhere had underestimated Ecgfrith as many people did and had lost the province of Lindsey as a result. The city of Lincoln and the plains around the monastery of Bardney were prizes indeed for the Northumbrian king. Wulfhere seemed to have gone downhill from then and he succumbed very easily to a fever. Whether it was because of the wearying journeys to battles in distant parts or the emotional toll of losing treasured territory no one knew but Wulfhere had rapidly declined in health since then and died. It seemed almost as though he had given up on life after his defeat.

Aethelred had heard about the impressive carved stone seat at Bamburgh used by the royal family as a throne. He wondered whether Ecgfrith would be sitting in state and whether he would be expected to bow to his future brother-in-law.

He need not have worried. Ecgfrith could not have been more welcoming. He strode forward to welcome him. Ecgfrith must have felt secure in the knowledge that he had got the better of the encounter with his brother. Looking at him now, Aethelred realised why his brother Wulfhere had underestimated him. He did not look as though he would be a difficult opponent but events had proved otherwise. Ecgfrith was now taller but was still of slight build and still had the same fine, almost delicate features that he had possessed as a boy. However, the years had been kind and he seemed to have found a new confidence and happiness.

Eormenberg, Ecgfrith's new wife, also gave them a warm welcome. She was a cheerful, plump and rather brisk woman, well dressed in colourful clothing. She could not have been more different from the previous wife of Ecgfrith who had, as far as Aethelred recalled, a slim build and a pale complexion with a sad expression. Ecgfrith had been much happier since this union. His first marriage to the much older woman Etheldreda had been a total disaster. Much relief was felt at his court when his first wife had retreated to a religious life, encouraged by Wilfred, her friend and priest. Etheldreda had felt an equal relief and was looking forward to the next stage of her life. This had left the door open for Ecgfrith to marry his mistress, Eormenberg.

Ecgfrith was keen that his sister should also know the happiness of a good marriage and he was not going to put any obstacles in her way. His distant memories of Aethelred were in no way unpleasant. He was conscious of the advantage of an alliance with Mercia. And maybe Osryth would be more fortunate than him in producing offspring. He was disappointed that after two years of marriage Eormenberg showed no signs of producing for him an heir. Otherwise their marriage was happy and fulfilling. Ecgfrith had secretly wondered whether the fact that he, the present Northumbrian king, was childless might have made the prospect of a union with a Northumbrian princess more attractive to Aethelred. He had encouraged Osryth to go to Tamworth; perhaps this was the outcome that he himself had secretly hoped for. It would certainly take away the pressure for him to produce an heir.

When he saw the young couple together he could see that his was not a marriage of convenience. They seemed genuinely fond of one another; their laughter and their whispered conversations together seemed to speak of their closeness.

Despite appearances Osryth was in turmoil. She wanted to confide in her brother her longstanding wish to bury what was left of Oswald's body. It may seem a very strange wish for someone contemplating marriage in the near future. However, she was reluctant to mention her plans for the treasure. She did not want either her brother or his wife to tell Aethelred about this part of her plan. Otherwise there may be no treasure or indeed maybe not even a marriage. That would be a tragedy. She may just mention the possibility of a pilgrimage taking her uncle's remains to Bardney.

After all, her brother of all people should understand her mission. An arm of Oswald's had been brought to Bamburgh by her father and was preserved in a silver casket and was said to have miraculous healing properties. It was said that Oswald's other arm had been picked up from the battlefield by a raven and it was then dropped on the ground not far away. An ash tree grew on that piece of ground and that too was reputed to have cured many people of their ailments. The well that gushed up in this spot also was said to have miraculous powers.

So when Ecgfrith asked her, 'Is all well?' she did mention her plans to go on a pilgrimage to Lincolnshire. He had heard her mention this many times in the past and knew their father had given the land at Bardney for that very purpose; however, he was surprised that she was contemplating this project in the near future. Osryth just reiterated that it was something that she must undertake and the sooner the better.

'Can you mention this to Aethelred – he guesses something is amiss and I just want him to know that once I have laid the remains of Oswald to rest then I will feel able to relax and concentrate more on being a proper wife to him.' She added, 'I know that it must seem very bad timing but I have never been so sure that I should undertake this.'

Ecgfrith knew how strong-willed his sister was. He knew that once she set her mind on something she would not easily be swayed. He agreed to try and explain this strange mission to Aethelred. It would not be easy to find the right words but at least it seemed as though his sister was trying to lay the past to rest.

And so Ecgfrith later explained to Aethelred, 'Osryth wants everything sorted out. She has wanted for a long while to transport the remains of her uncle to Bardney. It may seem strange to contemplate this at this happy time. But if you are both fortunate enough to have a family she knows she will not be able to travel so easily. She does feel that it is her Christian duty to complete this one unfinished task – I am sure that we will both understand that.'

Aethelred was relieved. He had thought that she was having second thoughts about actually marrying him.

This was so much easier to deal with. He replied, 'That is not a problem. I do not think that we can change the date of the wedding but a few days after the wedding she will be free to travel as she wishes. All the guests will have departed and I will have no objection. I will ensure that she can travel safely and send my most trusted retainers to look after her.' And he was relieved to find out the apparent reason for her sometimes abstracted and distant expression.

Later Osryth asked Ecgfrith about the possibility of using some of the skilled craftsmen from Wearmouth to create a memorial for their half-brother Alchfrid. 'I do not know why I am so concerned for him. Maybe he is still alive and just does not want to get in touch with his family. But something dreadful may have happened to him and I do think he should be remembered. My sister Aelfflaed has sometimes mentioned this to me.'

Ecgfrith agreed, saying that he should have thought of this earlier. Now his father Oswy was dead it would be easier to organise. He was aware of the tensions between the two at the Synod of Whitby. Ecgfrith said that he would send a message to Benedict Biscop, who he was sure would be amenable. The Gaulish craftsmen could be trusted to create an ornate cross and they would be asked inscribe the names of both Cyneberga and Alchfrid to commemorate both of them. He would ask for it to be made in the most long-lasting stone.

And while they stayed in the guest rooms at

Bamburgh, the prior of Lindisfarne, Cuthbert, visited Ecgfrith and paid his respects to the young couple. He was quite a regular visitor to Bamburgh. Despite his hardy appearance and weather-beaten complexion he had a gentle manner. He was good humoured and very good company. It was rumoured that he spent more time outdoors than in the monastery at Lindisfarne and would often spend the night outdoors in prayer. He would even pray in the sea itself. How refreshing, thought Aethelred who had loved to swim in the River Tame and its tributary the River Anker that passed by his home. Aethelred found Cuthbert quite inspiring. He had immediately put the young couple at their ease without any apparent effort. He seemed genuinely interested in their journey, particularly their adventures by boat, and was keen to hear about the places they had visited on the route. Osryth, who had known him for many years, regarded him as an old friend and was pleased to meet him again. They talked of their journey and the adventures that they had on the route. Cuthbert was interested to hear about the church in Monkwearmouth and the foreign craftsmen employed there.

'That may well be the future, you know. But that could not be further removed from the simplicity of Lindisfarne,' he said thoughtfully. The young couple knew that he had chosen a life of relative austerity. They were not surprised that this had endeared him to many country folk. It seemed apparent that even on this

short visit he treated everyone in the same manner; his
manner was no different with the servants as he was with
royalty. What was it about the Northumbrians, thought
Aethelred, that they seem to make no distinction of race
or class? For someone like Aethelred, who had not been
born first in line or expected to be a king but was now
thrust into the limelight, that was quite a relief. Both
Aethelred and Osryth enjoyed the company of Cuthbert
and they felt honoured when he invited them to visit
the holy island of Lindisfarne. They took advantage of
his invitation the day after his visit to Bamburgh. It was
a short trip by boat from Bamburgh; travelling by boat
meant that they did not need to worry about being cut
off by the tide. It could have been dangerous had they
arrived on foot and wanted to leave as the tide was
turning. As they approached the island of Lindisfarne
Osryth remembered the many times her father had
spoken of the Scottish island of Iona where he had spent
time as a youth. She wondered whether Lindisfarne was
similar to Iona. It was a beautiful and dramatic sight.
What was it about small islands that made them seem
holy? wondered Osryth.

The young couple were both impressed by the
monastery which was situated close to the sea. The
grass nearby seemed unusually green and lush and
they noticed there was the advantage of a natural water
supply. They sat in the picturesque abbey overlooking
the sea listening to the chanting of the monks and time

seemed to stand still. They were entranced. They wished that they could stay there longer. They knew that must return to Bamburgh before it got dark. Their boatman had become protective and wanted to take good care of his precious cargo. He did not want either of them to come to any harm on the rocks near the coastline.

The young couple both thought fleetingly of how fitting a wedding would be in this place. But Aethelred knew the importance of keeping one's word; he had already decided where the ceremony should be held and he was sure that it would be a mistake to change his mind. He had told the priest Winfrith of his intentions to marry in Tamworth. And even though Winfrith himself was an equable man any change of mind might be seen as a weakness. He also recalled being warned by his brother Wulfhere about the Northumbrian royal family. Their elder brother Paeda had died in Northumbria when surrounded by the family of Osryth. That was many years ago but it would do no harm to be cautious. The wedding would be safer on his home ground. He did not want to put himself in any danger.

They returned to Bamburgh and the next few days passed pleasantly. They told Ecgfrith about their plans for the wedding and their hope that he and Eormenberg would attend. Ecgfrith was told about the marriage settlement, the morning gift, but he did not query the source of the treasure. Nor did Osryth disclose her plans for it.

CHAPTER 3
THE WEDDING

AD 675   **MAY 15TH**

*'...An attendant stood by
with a decorated pitcher, pouring bright
 helpings of mead...'* Lines 494-496

*'...he examined the hilt,
that relic of old times. It was engraved all over'*
Lines 1687-1688

*'In pure gold inlay on the sword-guards
there were rune-markings correctly incised,
stating and recording for whom the sword
had been first made and ornamented
with its scroll-worked hilt...'* **Lines 1694-1698** *Beowulf*

The day of the wedding dawned bright. The royal
feasting hall at Tamworth was decorated with garlands.
Tables were heavily laden. Animals had been slaughtered
and an ox roast was being prepared. A large bonfire
had been built up in the courtyard for that purpose.
The kitchen was busy with preparation. The serving
staff were happy to prepare for a wedding ceremony;

too often in times past they had to provide supplies for the seemingly endless excursions to battle. They were curious to see the Northumbrian contingent; Osryth had stayed with them a few weeks previously. She had been treated much like part of the family and it was obvious to them then that there was an understanding between her and Aethelred. News of a wedding had come as no surprise to them. Nevertheless some of the thegns had glum faces. It was difficult to forget the recent war that had been waged and the companions that they had lost in Northumbria.

The day before the wedding, cauldrons of water had been heated over the fire and a wooden bathtub was provided for the bride and groom in their respective rooms. A bath was a luxury only enjoyed a few times of the year. Tradition dictated that the wedding couple did not see each other the day before the ceremony and this would be no exception.

Osryth had travelled back from Whitby with her mother and sister and Anna her attendant. After several tiring days on the road the party from Whitby had arrived at Tamworth the day before the wedding. All of them were glad when the journey came to an end. The jolting of the wagon and the evenings in wayside inns had left them weary. They had wondered at some stages of the journey whether they would be late for the ceremony.

Anna was looking forward to this event. She had never been to a wedding before. She had been looking after the wedding dress and the flowers. On their arrival at Tamworth she carried the dress carefully from the wagon and then returned for the bunches of freshly picked flowers, some given to them on the route by local people intrigued and pleased by the thought of a wedding. The elaborately embroidered dress had been draped carefully over a bench in the wagon and was still in good shape; fortunately it had not rained, otherwise the dress might then have got damp even under the canopy of the wagon.

Eanfled felt a strange sensation as she entered what had been the home of her old enemy, Penda. She was curious to see the building which before now she had only glimpsed from a distance when handing over her ten year old son. It was more pleasant than she had remembered. The royal hall was large in size and not far away was a small religious community where guest rooms were provided. Two rivers, a main river and its tributary flowed peacefully nearby. It seemed strange that preparations for so many battles must have taken place here in the past. She hoped that everything would turn out well for Aethelred and Osryth and that their marriage would not be blighted by the troubles of times gone by.

Osryth was grateful for the chance to wash herself after several days on the road. She immersed herself in the bathwater and lay there until she felt totally cleansed. She felt soothed in the heat and comfort of the warm water. She lay there wondering about how her new life would turn out. She hoped that her future would be trouble-free and fulfilling.

Thoughts flitted through her mind. Osryth had got to know Aethelred well over the past few months. She wondered what emotions Aethelred was feeling and whether he enjoyed a bath as much as she did. He was such a practical man. She could see him in her mind's eye briskly washing himself before quickly drying himself off and then shaving his face before washing and drying and combing his fair hair. He was very orderly; having grown up with so many brothers and sisters he had not had much time to himself.

Osryth had long felt sorry that Aethelred's mother had passed away a few years previously; it was sad that she was not here to witness her son's special day. That would make the occasion all the more poignant for Aethelred, she reflected. Osryth would have liked to have met his mother. She had heard a good account of her from her own mother, Eanfled, who had met her when she had been forced by Penda to hand over her son. That had not made the giving up of her son any easier, but at least she had seen some kindness in the household and had felt reassured. At this wedding ceremony no one would miss Penda himself, least of all the Northumbrian contingent, particularly those who remembered the endless wars that were waged.

As Osryth lay soaking, her mother and sister and Anna arranged her clothes for the following morning.

They worked at a small trestle table and prepared a circlet of flowers to place on her head; then they arranged a bouquet of flowers for Osryth. They made posies of lilies-of-the-valley for Aelfflaed and Anna, who would be bridesmaids. They busied themselves in this way until Osryth got out of her bath, dried herself and put on her nightgown. The bouquet and the smaller bunches of flowers were placed in a bucket of water. They smiled at her. Osryth looked at what they had been doing. She was pleased that they had gone to this trouble. She felt refreshed after her long bath and later slept soundly.

The morning of the wedding soon arrived. Osryth's mother and sister and attendant helped to dress her. Osryth looked resplendent in her flowing dress, which was embroidered with swirling patterns of blue and gold. The circlet of fresh flowers was placed on her hair, which was braided and coiled on the top of her head. She carried a bouquet of bluebells, meadowsweet and cow parsley tied up with a ribbon. The scent from these filled the air around her. Aelfflaed felt a pang of sadness; her sister looked beautiful and she hoped that all would be well with her union. Having recently enjoyed the company of Osryth, she was sad that they would soon be parted again. 'I do hope that all will be well with you both and that we see you again before long,' she murmured, almost under her breath. She did not want to cast a shadow over the celebrations.

Osryth walked into the royal hall with her attendants.

Aethelred was wearing his finest clothes and a purple cloak. He also wore his sword; this was an important part of the ceremony. Osryth felt a surge of pride that this tall suitor would soon be her husband. They smiled at one another; both felt confident when they saw each other that they would have a long and happy marriage.

Osryth's brother Ecgfrith and his new wife arrived just in time for the ceremony. Their journey had been long and arduous and they were glad to have arrived and curious to see the royal hall in Tamworth. Ecgfrith thought that it looked smaller and less grim than he remembered. He was here under much happier circumstances, he realised. The younger brother of Ecgfrith and Osryth, Aelfwine, entered the hall with them. He was an athletic-looking young man in his late teens. He was already being given responsibility as a royal and was a popular character both at home with his family and further afield. He seemed full of life and looked around him curiously. Osryth was very pleased that he had also made the journey. He was a favourite of everyone. She was sure that her younger brother and Aethelred would become good friends.

At the ceremony Ecgfrith preceded his sister as she went to meet Aethelred. Osryth was given away by Ecgfrith, a poignant moment for their mother, Eanfled. How proud Oswy would have been of his handsome children, now so grown up, she thought. Osryth's nephew and nieces were also dressed in their finest clothes. Aethelred himself was overcome by emotion as he saw his close relatives; he looked at Osric, his oldest nephew, the son of his eldest sister, Cyneberga, standing tall and straight and he was filled with pride. He smiled at Cyneberga, who had travelled from Castor near Peterborough where she had become abbess. Despite the warmongering in the past there were many similarities between the two families, including their Christian faith. It was strange that despite their upbringing all the children of Penda had embraced Christianity. And now Aethelred was the third of his siblings to marry one of the offspring of Oswy. This was beginning to be part of a pattern. Aethelred smiled.

Osryth, his bride, was indeed looking beautiful and Aethelred could not believe his good fortune.

As was the custom, Ecgfrith carried an ancestral sword. He gave it to Osryth, who handed it over in turn to Aethelred, saying, 'This sword which I give you is yours to keep and to hand down to our descendants.'

She added, 'You must carry a sword to keep us safe and to keep us secure in our homes.' She stumbled slightly on the words. The sight of the weapons may well upset her mother. The sword was an ornate, heavy weapon which sparkled with jewels. In turn the valuable Mercian sword that Aethelred wore was handed to Ecgfrith. The wedding ring had been placed on this sword and then the ring was handed to Osryth, who placed it on the fourth finger of her left hand.

This ceremony indicated that Osryth would be well protected. This brought tears to the eyes of Eanfled, who remembered the battles of time past. She recalled the sadness she had felt when her son Ecgfrith was a young boy and had been handed over as a hostage to Penda's wife after one of the many wars. The two boys Ecgfrith and Aethelred had grown up together like brothers for several years, and now here they were actually exchanging swords in this traditional ceremony and would soon become brothers-in-law.

The rest of the ceremony flowed smoothly. Osryth handed over a wedding ring to Aethelred and the couple said their vows in front of Bishop Winfrith, who had officiated at Lichfield in times gone by. He gave the couple his blessing. He was an elderly stooping cleric in colourful robes who was very pleased to be present at this wedding. He loved to see the excitement and the formality of the actual ceremony. He thought that no ill could come of it; after all, the young couple had both converted to Christianity. He had not sought the permission of the archbishop because he knew that this might not be given. Winfrith himself was about to be replaced in Lichfield, and too much tragic history had been played out by the two families. This was the third marriage taking place between the offspring of Penda and of Oswy. Not all had ended well. Osryth's half-sister was actually suspected of being involved in the murder in Northumbria of her husband, Aethelred's eldest brother, Paeda. He would have made a good king, it was thought by many. And this had cast a shadow on the character of Oswy's children. It was fortunate that Osryth's older half-brother Alchfrid, had a happy marriage with Aethelred's older sister. They had married at the instigation of Oswy and Penda, who could see the advantage in the two kingdoms being united. But unfortunately Alchfrid had disappeared; he was either dead or in exile. Maybe he had died in the plague which had swept the country eleven years ago. The plague had swept through many communities and was no respecter of persons. He could have died on his journey back from the Synod of Whitby and no one be the wiser. There would have been a hasty burial and no ceremony. He and his retainers may all have perished. It was rumoured that he had exiled himself to a small monastery in a remote area in the north of the Rheged region. It was known that he had had a disagreement with his father. No one knew for sure. Cyneberga, the wife of Alchfrid, had a long-suffering look. She hoped that there would be a happier outcome for her brother Aethelred than for herself. She was pleased and proud for her children to attend the wedding. The death of Paeda and the disappearance of Alchfrid were not good omens but perhaps this young couple getting married could overcome the difficulties of a marriage between families who had been at war. There was still hope.

After the actual wedding rites, in a final dramatic flourish, Aethelred handed over the heavy keys of the royal hall to Osryth. She received them with a smile. One of them she knew was the key to the strongroom where the treasure was kept. The treasure would be given to Osryth the next morning in front of witnesses. Osryth did not let the keys go out of sight. They were too heavy to keep on her sash so she handed them to Aelfflaed during the reception for safe keeping. The ceremony was declared over and the celebrations could begin.

Casks of ale and flagons of mead were carried to the tables to toast the young couple.

The minstrels struck up a merry tune and as the final preparations for the feast took place there was dancing around the mead hall. Figures were swirling around and Osryth danced her first dance with her new husband, happy that all had gone well. As more joined in she could see her young attendant Anna dancing with one of Aethelred's young noblemen and she smiled. Perhaps life in Tamworth would be more exciting than she had thought.

The feast then took place. Everyone was glad to sit down. Those from Northumbria had never seen such a meal with so many different courses. Long trestle tables had been placed around the royal feasting hall. The fire in the centre of the room burned brightly. Occasionally a gust of wind would send smoke spiralling through the room rather than out of the roof. It stung the eyes and accounted for the tears of some of those present.

But merriment was the keynote. And the speeches

flowed freely; the mead and the ale had loosened the tongues of those speaking. And as the jugglers entertained in the background the wedding party relaxed more and more.

It was a long day with all the celebration and feasting. Osryth was glad when the time came to retire. Everything had become a bit of a blur and she was giddy with the drink and the dancing. Aethelred was delighted that all had gone so well and they said goodnight to their guests and went together to their chamber. They were cheered on their way by the crowd. Both were tired but exhilarated by all the festivities.

Next morning Osryth tried out the large key to the strongroom for the first time.

Aethelred accompanied her. 'And now is the time for the treasure to be handed over,' he said and smiled warmly. The wedding had gone well and he was fulfilling his part of the bargain. A large linen bag was produced. It was carried to one of the refectory tables and emptied. As was the custom many of the valuables had been broken in parts or twisted to symbolise the division of property on marriage. The remnants sparkled in the reflection of the still-glowing embers of the fire. They caught the light and Osryth gasped at the gold and the jewels. The cloisonné and gold filigree work was intricate and beautiful. And so many items, albeit small and light. They must be worth a fortune. They looked like items taken off swords. But it was disconcerting to think that these sparkling fragments had been used in battle. There were many pommel caps and hilts; these remnants must have come from over a hundred swords. And a gold cross with a garnet. And another item with some words inscribed in Latin; she discovered from Aelfflaed that this was a prayer asking God to ensure that their enemies flee. It may well have related back to the battle of Maserfield and even further back. Osryth gave a slight shudder at the thought that Aethelred must have retained so many blades. Why would he do this? Was he intending to follow the example of his father and continually wage war? Would he change with marriage? Some of the items looked familiar and she could not help but wonder if it was the remnants of battle that her father had gleaned after his brother had been killed. She recalled hearing that her father had handed over some treasure to Penda when he was at his wit's end as to how to deter him from waging war. Her father had even handed over her brother Ecgfrith at one stage to appease Penda. He had been cared for by Penda's wife. How difficult that must have been for her mother, Eanfled. Not only to give up a fortune but also to relinquish a son, not knowing what might happen to him. Maybe it was her father Oswy who had detached the pommel caps from the blades. He would not want to hand weapons over to his long-time enemy.

A premonition of trouble to come could not be banished, however, and Osryth remained quiet for the rest of the day much to Aethelred's concern.

PART 2
SUMMER

CHAPTER 4
JOURNEY TO OSWESTRY

AD 675 1 JUNE

'... There were many other
heirlooms heaped inside the earth-house
because long ago, with deliberate care,
some forgotten person had deposited the whole
rich inheritance of a high-born race
in this ancient cache...' **Lines 2231-2236 Beowulf**

The summer months had arrived. The warmth of the midday sun brightened the atmosphere and the showers that fell were a welcome relief for the dry ground.

Osryth's relatives were about to depart. Her mother and sister were concerned that the Abbess Hilda might need their help at Whitby. She had been too frail to make the journey to Mercia. Everyone knew that Hilda's health was deteriorating. The fortnight in the royal hall at Tamworth had passed quickly. 'Where has the time gone?' Osryth wondered aloud to her family. And they knew that a long time might elapse before they next met. 'Do travel safely and give my greetings to those back in Whitby,' Osryth said, her eyes beginning to glimmer with tears. Who was to know what adventures might befall each of them and when they may all meet again?

Ten days earlier Osryth, her mother and her sister had all gone on an early morning outing. Osryth had used the key to the strongroom and removed a heavy linen bag before Aethelred was awake. The three women had crept silently out of their accommodation in Tamworth just before the dawn broke. Osryth had gone to the stables where she hitched the cart to the smallest horse. It was not easy to manage the horse and cart without disturbing anyone. She wore a shorter tunic than usual; this was the only practical way to ride a horse. Even so she had to hitch up the skirt of the tunic to avoid it getting caught. Her mother and sister travelled in the cart, looking after the linen bag. None of them wanted to be seen. They buried the bag in a shallow dip near the crossroads of Watling Street and Ryknild Street; there was a raised ridge near thick woodland so there should be no problem recalling the area, they thought. Eanfled had taken off the gold necklace she had been wearing at the wedding. It was a valuable item set with amber. It was placed on a branch of a tree overhanging the spot and two large stakes had been placed in the newly dug earth as markers. They had all washed the soil off their hands in the stream nearby. No one had noticed their coming and going, not even the stable boy. Only a stray magpie had been watching.

Aelfflaed and her mother were happy to help Osryth. They had overcome their qualms about the secretive nature of this mission. The three women were all happy at the thought that some treasure would be taken to the abbey at Bardney. It was not unusual for the bodies of warriors to be buried with their treasure. And surely the contents of the linen sack now rightfully belonged to Osryth. Not only had it been given to Osryth but they were convinced that it had a connection with King Oswy in the distant past. The two young women wished to honour their father and uncle and Osryth looked forward to her pilgrimage to Lincolnshire. She reassured her mother and sister, 'As you know a morning gift becomes the property of the bride as soon as it is given and I am free to dispose of it as I think fit.' Despite that, no one had the slightest inclination to inform Aethelred. He need not know what was intended. They realised it would not be easy to confide in him. Too many wars had been fought between their respective families. The thought of them caused Eanfled and her daughters to shudder.

Hiding the linen sack was one way not to draw attention to it for the time being. Osryth planned to retrieve it on her return journey from Oswestry. She and her retainers could take it with the remains of her uncle and place it in Bardney Abbey as her father had wished.

Aethelred had spent the last week and more hunting wild boars with his thegns, returning each afternoon proud of his spoils. The dead boars were dragged in a cart back to the royal hall. They would provide enough meat to last the royal household for weeks.

After the wedding the excitement subsided and the royal hall seemed much more subdued. Even Aethelred's nieces and nephews were quieter than usual and then after a few days they left with their mother back to Peterborough. Osryth was ready for a new adventure. Drinking mead every day as was customary after getting married was good. She appreciated her new husband and her marriage pleased her. She looked at Aethelred with wonder and could not believe her good fortune. Sometimes she wanted to pinch herself to check that this was real. However, despite this newfound happiness she was getting restless and wanted a new challenge.

She decided to carry out her mission to collect the remains of Oswald's body. She would have liked Aethelred to accompany her but he had become increasingly engrossed with his hunting and his affairs of state. He had neglected these during his courtship. Osryth felt a degree of relief. At least he would not find out about the buried treasure.

And he helped her plan her itinerary via the bishop's house in Brewood, then on to the hall of his family in Atcham where his sister Cyneswith resided and then onto Oswestry. He advised that they should never be too far from the rivers; the horses would need not only food but also water. The River Penk and the River Severn would be useful stopping points. She and her retinue could be looked after in comfort at the places he suggested. They would need ample supplies of food and small casks of beer would be stored in the cart. It was not always possible to find clean and fresh water to drink. Aethelred drew a rough diagram of the proposed route and Osryth was relieved that it was quite straightforward and the main part of the journey would be along Watling Street.

Osryth knew that once in Oswestry she must find the remains of her uncle. After he had been killed in battle his body had been hacked into pieces by Penda's men. Her father Oswy had often related how Oswald's torso and legs were kept in a casket wrapped in a purple and gold flag near to where he had fallen. When Oswy had visited the battlefield some time later he had ensured that his men had built a stone monument to commemorate his brother and had placed the casket inside. He took away an arm and the severed head, both of which had been placed on stakes by Penda's men in a cruel pagan ritual. Oswy had taken these back to Bamburgh with him. They were placed in separate silver caskets. It had been the cruellest of deaths for Oswald, who it was said had prayed for the souls of the soldiers as he approached battle. Despite the mutilation after his death his remains were said to have miraculous healing powers not only for humans but also for animals. Many examples were cited.

Over thirty years had elapsed since the battle of Maserfield. The casket with his bones would not be heavy. Just a few bones and no doubt a faded and frayed flag, but nevertheless precious not only to Osryth but also to many others, she hoped. The healing powers of her uncle's body had become widely reported. She would visit the well which had sprung up after her uncle's death and where it was rumoured a raven had dropped one of his arms.

On her return journey from Oswestry, Osryth intended to collect the buried treasure from the crossroads near the forest and transport it along in the same wagon to Bardney. She would have to be careful that the thegns did not ask too many questions. It did not seem as though anything could go wrong.

Her family had now left the royal hall at Tamworth. As close relatives of the royal family Osryth's mother and sister were given a large retinue to accompany them back to Whitby. Her mother appeared reflective and said, 'It seems strange that the soldiers of years past who had been our enemies are now our protectors.' And yet she was secretly pleased to have some protection from raiders and wild animals on their long journey back to Whitby. The horses were the finest that could be spared by Aethelred. They would be able to travel the distance comfortably and at a good speed.

And Osryth herself, as a royal wife, was offered a number of loyal thegns to accompany her on her journey. She departed two days later. Her husband was anxious to ensure her safety too. He provided six thegns in total, two to go ahead and warn of any danger, two to stay at the rear and check that all was safe and two on horseback pulling the wagon where Osryth and Anna, her attendant, sat. Osryth was aware of her privileged position. Not many women, even of her rank, would be able to travel so easily. However, despite the many cushions piled up it was not the most comfortable of journeys. Potholes were plentiful on the old Roman road and both Osryth and Anna would have liked to change places with the thegns looking after them and ride on horseback. But that would not be allowed and so the two women tried to get into as restful a position as possible, frequently changing their position and rearranging the throws. Both women were youthful and did not have to contend with the stiffness of advancing years. Osryth reflected that it was just as well that the Abbess Hilda had not attempted the arduous journey to Mercia. They knew that even for young women such as them it would be a long gruelling pilgrimage to find Oswald's bones and take them to Bardney Abbey.

They passed the small settlement of houses made of wattle and daub with their thatched roofs. Some had small wisps of smoke curling out of the roofs. It seemed unreal. It was still chilly in the early morning and the breath from the horses steamed in the cold air. Slowly the sun filtered through the mist. And the shadows of the trees along Watling Street formed a trellis along the track.

Osryth looked around with interest. Every part of the track looked similar to the last section and it was intersected in several places by wide paths. She had a sudden moment of panic. How could she be sure where she and her sister and her mother had buried the treasure? She thought of the many items, the gold cross with the red garnet and its intricate pattern of gold, the elaborate depictions of eagles and seahorses and the many jewelled remnants taken from swords. Her heart sank. What if she could not remember on her return journey exactly where the linen bag had been placed? she thought to herself. She told herself not to panic. And then she remembered the fragments of a helmet in the hoard. Was that what Oswald had been wearing when he was killed? She recalled her father telling her that Oswald was too much a target at the battle of Maserfield because of his distinctive headwear. Nothing would now bring him back, but how good it would be to honour the abbey at Bardney with not only the remains of her uncle but also the valuable remnants of battle.

'Is everything alright?' asked Anna anxiously.

Osryth was interrupted from her reverie. 'Everything is fine,' she replied, wondering inwardly whether this journey was going to be as straightforward as she had hoped.

Osryth tried to focus on other matters. She had noticed that Anna and Edric seemed to sparkle in each other's company. Was he not the handsome young nobleman who had danced with Anna at the wedding party at Tamworth? They seemed well suited and Osryth was pleased. If Anna settled down in Mercia perhaps Osryth herself would not feel lonely.

After that the journey seemed to pass quickly. The

thegns knew their way to the country retreat of Bishop Winfrith set as it was on high wooded ground. Bishop's Wood in Brewood - the names spoke for themselves. When they arrived everyone was tired. At least there had been no scares on the journey, no brigands and no wolves. So, after a good meal prepared by the staff everyone went to their rooms and fell fast asleep. The men all stayed in one dormitory and again Osryth had the company of Anna. She wished that she could take her into her confidence and tell her about the buried treasure. It was on the tip of her tongue to describe her plan. But the less anyone knew about it the less likely it was that the treasure would disappear. She did not know who to trust among the Mercian noblemen.

The next morning the rain started falling. This was an unpleasant shock. Steady drizzle and damp underfoot. The small casks of water on the wagon seemed unnecessary. There was water everywhere. The horses trudged wearily along the damp ground. It was a long way to Atcham. Watling Street became much wider and better kept up as the journey progressed. The next stop would be very welcome. By now everyone was damp. The spare clothes in the leather holdalls would be needed and the damp ones would have to dry out in front of the fire. No doubt the kitchens would be kept warm particularly for visitors, she thought. As the rain was subsiding the party sheltered for a short while at the Roman city of Wroxeter, which was a very short distance from Watling

Street. What a pity that the fine sandstone buildings there were crumbling and the area was practically deserted. Osryth tried to imagine it as a bustling city. She had heard it was one of the finest cities that the Romans had built. It was the fourth largest in the country. She looked round in wonder and curiosity. Some ox carts were standing by, laden with grey and red sandstone. She was told that these were destined for the building of the nearby church in Atcham. She reflected aloud, 'Would it not be wonderful if that church could be dedicated to one of our people, perhaps Bishop Eata of Melrose who introduced Cuthbert to Lindisfarne? It would mean that our visit here is marked and remembered for centuries to come. I will speak to Aethelred about it. I am sure that we would both be very happy if that could be done. Then the two kingdoms will seem even more united.'

It was late afternoon when they arrived at Atcham. They were welcomed and beckoned in out of the rain. The horses were able to shelter in the stables adjoining the hall. There was a large oblong feasting hall made of wood. A blazing fire had been lit in the centre of the feasting hall. The long table was laden with warm food, boiled meat, cabbage and swede with melted cheese. Osryth thought of her husband. She felt grateful. He must have sent a messenger ahead of them to forewarn the household of their arrival. Damp clothes were changed and replaced. After the meal, as was the custom with their visitors, she was given an acorn to plant in the grounds. It was still light and the rain had subsided. She walked with Anna and Cyneswith, Aethelred's sister, to a far corner of the estate. She found a patch of land near a small tributary of the wide river flowing by. She could see the mound of a prominent hill a few miles away to the other side of Wroxeter.

'At least that is a good landmark,' she commented aloud. It was a shame that there were not more landmarks in Mercia, she thought to herself. She planted the acorn deep in the moist ground, her hands becoming covered in soil. She washed her hands in the small stream. This was the second time she had done this in the recent past, she reflected, thinking of the buried treasure, and how she had to wash her hands then. She wondered how the small acorn would grow and whether the result of this small action would last through the centuries. The damp ground would no doubt assist the little seedling to germinate and grow. It was strange to think that the tiny acorn may outlive all those that she knew. And it pleased her to have such close contact with the earth; as a royal there were not many opportunities to feel so grounded. 'I feel like this is a new beginning,' she said to her companions as they walked back to the hall. She herself was not sure what she was referring to and whether she meant her marriage or the planting of the acorn or the journey to find the remains of her uncle. It did not matter, she told herself. All these recent experiences were part of a new chapter in her life.

Aethelred's sister offered her overnight accommodation and would have been happy for them all to stay longer. But this was regretfully declined; one night would have to be enough. The beds were comfortable and the feather down in the mattress was soft and warm; the wooden-framed beds were placed well above the grounds and smelt of lavender and mint. How sensible, Osryth thought, as she lay down to sleep. The thought flitted through her mind that she could try to introduce these improvements to Tamworth. But Tamworth would never appear so welcoming and hospitable; it was a functional fortress with furniture to match. Trestle tables and long benches for a dining area and beds on the floor with mattresses of straw were the best the Mercian palace could offer.

Osryth soon fell asleep and slept soundly; she would have welcomed a longer stay in this beautiful parkland near the River Severn. However, she knew that their mission could not be delayed. The men may become impatient. She did not feel entirely comfortable with the Mercian thegns. They kept their own company and only spoke to her if addressed directly. They were polite but distant and she desperately hoped that she was not leading them on a hopeless mission looking for the remains of her uncle. She would be mortified if the casket containing his bones could not be found. The reaction of the men would be difficult for her to bear. Sometimes she got the impression that they were willing her to fail in this project. She was very glad of the company of Anna and glad too to get to know Aethelred's sister. At breakfast she decided that this was the opportunity to speak about the new church being built nearby and discuss a possible dedication to Eata. This suggestion was well received. 'We will certainly consider this and many thanks for the suggestion - I can see it would be a good way of linking far distant parts of the country. You must tell me more about this Bishop Eata,' said Cyneswith. She was pleased to discover a way of honouring their guests from the north east of the country and fulfilling the wishes of the beautiful new wife of Aethelred. And Osryth related all that she knew about Eata of Melrose.

Next morning dawned bright and clear. As the party departed on horseback Osryth looked back at the large wooden hall surrounded by a moat. She had not expected such a welcome. It had been a very pleasant surprise, and her retinue were pleased with a good night's accommodation. They woke refreshed and in good humour. Now came the last stretch of the journey. Osryth said a little prayer. If only she could carry out her mission successfully she would go back to a happy marriage and all would be well.

In the evening they arrived in Oswestry with the shadows of Oswestry hillfort looming a short distance away. The well was clearly signposted in the centre of town. A small monument had been built nearby; a cross on the roof was an indication. Was this the location of the casket? To her amazement it was. And, as she had anticipated, the purple and gold flag was faded but at least it was still in one piece and wrapped several times around the casket. This really was too good to be true. Perhaps it proved the power of prayer, Osryth reflected.

The thegns were relieved that this was not a fruitless journey. 'We are glad that our journey has not been in vain,' said the lead thegn, a man of usually serious demeanour. He smiled with the satisfaction of one with a mission accomplished. The men lifted the casket from its resting place. As anticipated it was not heavy. It was placed gently on the wagon. A few of the local people stood around curiously. They were not going to question this impressively dressed and well-armed group. Osryth showed the cross she wore around her neck. This was obviously a religious pilgrimage; the observers looked relieved.

That evening as they stayed in a local inn not far from Watling Street Osryth lay wide awake. Her mind was racing. She could not believe that she had been successful in this part of her quest. 'I hope that the return journey works out as well,' she said to her attendant. There was no reply. Anna was fast asleep. Osryth tossed and turned and it was the early morning before she drifted off to sleep.

CHAPTER 5
MISSING TREASURE

'They let the ground keep that ancestral treasure,
gold under gravel, gone to earth,
as useless to men now as it ever was'
Lines 3166-3168 *Beowulf*

It was time for the return journey. The thegns laughed and chatted together, pleased that they had accomplished this part of their undertaking. They would be well rewarded by Aethelred on their return. Many forays had been undertaken in the past; these noblemen knew the lie of the land.

'We are retracing our steps along Watling Street?' queried Osryth, thinking of the treasure she must reclaim. How could she explain her reasons to these men accompanying her? And could they be trusted?

'No,' said the leader of the group, who until now had been taciturn and quiet. He added, 'No, we know a quicker route. We will make our way through Hodnet and Uttoxeter toward Chesterfield. And then travel eastward towards Lincoln and Bardney.' He then looked at her directly. 'And I understand that Aethelred will be expecting you back in Tamworth in a week or so.'

The thegns were not used to accepting orders from a

woman and Osryth did not want to challenge the route devised by her retinue. She felt alarmed. The point of burying the treasure was lost. She had imagined that they would travel back along Watling Street. But how was she to explain this? She would have to retrieve the hoard another time. Her heart sank as she realised that those in Bardney may well be expecting to receive not only the remains of Oswald but also some treasure to bury alongside him. She remembered with rising panic that her mother had said that she would write to the religious community in Bardney to tell them of her visit.

The thegns looked at her suspiciously. They wondered why she was looking so concerned. They could not understand why she had undertaken this journey so soon after her marriage. What was it that she was concealing from her husband? They had heard rumours that more than a decade previously Aethelred's older brother Paeda had been murdered in Northumbria within a year of his marriage to Osryth's half-sister. Some said it was with the connivance of the latter. The men kept their counsel but looked wary.

The horses seemed to have a new spurt of energy. The weather was clear and sharp and the mud and the deep puddles were drying up. After an early start in the morning the small settlement of Hodnet was quickly reached and a hearty meal was eaten there. Aethelred's sister had been generous with the fresh supplies she had given to them for their journey. All the group were pleased with such ample provisions. They stocked up their water supply from the large lake in pleasant parkland nearby.

'We have a long journey ahead. It will take a few days to get to Bardney. Better to stay here and then at Uttoxeter and then travel onwards towards Lincoln,' said the lead thegn.

And so the group travelled on. The landscape was monotonous, trees and more trees, mixed vegetation and scrub lining the road. Osryth adjusted the cushions around her and rested her head. Before long she was dozing and despite her efforts to stay awake she fell fast asleep. When they reached Uttoxeter she awoke with a jolt. She was looking forward to staying in a farmstead among the rolling countryside there. She was conscious that the next day she must try to remain more alert. Anna was also looking forward to their next sojourn. It could be time to have another wash and a change of clothes. Her curly dark hair had become tangled and matted and her face was dusty with the travelling. It was hard to stay clean and fresh on such a long journey. At least they could generally remain dry in the covered wagon attached to the horses.

The plentiful supply of clean remnants of fabric they carried enabled them to wash their faces and hands on a daily basis but they longed to bathe in fresh water. It was difficult for women to travel, Osryth reflected. A long tunic with a cloak over it fixed either side by a brooch, as was the custom, was bound to be cumbersome. It would have been almost impossible to ride a horse dressed in such a way. Sometimes they envied the men with their short tunics. Everything seemed more straightforward for them.

During the next day they passed a small lake near to a farm track in the undulating landscape. The weather was warm and humid and so the decision was made to stop for a while. Bathing in a cold pool was a rare treat but a shock to the system. They needed to get clean. The men took little time to get into the water in their short tunics and were soon racing against each other. It was the happiest she had seen them. They obviously enjoyed the exercise. She had not realised that they were so competitive. The women took longer to get ready. They chose a distant part of the pool close to some trees. Getting ready required some complicated dressing and undressing. But at least it was a chance to get clean. Both women could swim; they had learned this skill when young in the sea close to their homes. Swimming in a small lake in their linen shifts would keep them warmer than just a cold dip. And it was one way of washing their undergarments. Fresh ones would have to be found from their spare clothes while the damp ones dried. Anna was able to comb her curly dark hair with the small ivory comb they carried. And Osryth shook out her long golden locks as they dried. All felt refreshed. And then it was time to travel on.

And each of the days merged into each other. Osryth felt helpless. She said to Anna, 'The sooner this journey is over the better.'

Anna replied, 'I expect that you must be looking forward to returning home.' This shocked Osryth. It was still very hard to think of Tamworth as home. The contrast between the dramatic coastlines of Bamburgh and the much gentler landscapes of Mercia could not have been greater. It made her feel homesick.

'I look forward to seeing my husband again,' replied Osryth. 'And I do hope that I start to regard Tamworth as my home.'

'I miss my home in Whitby very much too,' said Anna, 'This is the first time that I have been away for a long period. But it is an adventure nevertheless.' And she smiled.

And no doubt made more enjoyable to Anna by the friendship that she had formed with Edric, Osryth thought to herself.

But Osryth was puzzled. Why had she not been warned by Aethelred about the different route she would be taking on her return? He had been so clear about the various places she would visit. Did he know that she would be going on a diversion through the centre of Mercia towards Lincoln? Did he know about the hidden treasure and was he taking revenge? Or was this just his men who wanted to assert their authority? And would she dare complain about them? Only time would tell.

CHAPTER 6
PILGRIMAGE TO BARDNEY

*'A light appeared and the place brightened
the way the sky does when heaven's candle
is shining clearly...'* **Lines 1570-1572 Beowulf**

The journey from Oswestry to Bardney seemed endless.
The jolting of the wagon, the breaks they took for a
small meal and the quick comfort breaks in the wooded
areas adjacent to the road were repeated day after day.
Each one of the small group of travellers heaved a sigh
of relief when they eventually approached the large
settlement of Lincoln. Their final destination was only
a few miles away. As they approached the settlement
they could see its dramatic outline. Excitement grew.
They went through a narrow Roman arch and the horses
clattered up the steep hill at the centre of the town. They
looked at the vast landscape stretching out. Below them
they could see a narrow irregular grid of cobbled streets.
There were remains of Roman buildings and clusters of
new edifices. 'Look over there,' said Osryth pointing
eastward. 'I am sure that Bardney is in that direction,
close to a river.' She was worn out after the long day's
travelling but elated at the prospect of fulfilling her
mission. The Mercian thegns had after all been going
in the right direction. She had wondered several times

whether they were correct about the route.

'We know this area well,' said the lead thegn. 'If you recall, this area was under our control until just over a year ago.' He looked gloomy. Osryth guessed that he must be referring to her brother Ecgfrith's success in the battle against Wulfhere; Ecgfrith's main prize was the province of Lindsey. Before that the province had belonged to Mercia. It was difficult to be in the company of men who had fought against her brother in the recent past. Most of the time their conversation turned around the practicalities of travelling and most of them were good natured but occasionally, as now, Osryth felt as though she had to tread carefully. It would be better not to mention her brother, she decided.

Lincoln was a picturesque town with traces of buildings from the Roman era. One building in particular caught their attention, a fine stone-built church that was in good order apart from being completely open to the sky. All of the roof was missing; birds darted in and out of their nests in the narrow window apertures. The group of travellers watched them as they sat there for a while on a bench there; they marvelled at the natural light that flooded the edifice. An old well was situated close by. 'That will be useful to fill up our flagons,' said one of the thegns, 'and it will provide us now with much needed drinks of water. I am quite thirsty. The water may taste better if it comes from a holy well as surely this must be being so close to a church.' They all looked relieved that their water supply would be replenished. They had not passed many rivers or even small streams in recent days on their route.

As they sat in the old stone church they noticed the figure of a white-haired and white-bearded pilgrim. He walked with the aid of a stick but otherwise seemed to be in good health. He approached the group and asked them their business. 'We are on our way to the abbey in Bardney,' said one of the thegns. 'We hope that it is not too far away.'

'Not far, just a few miles from here,' said the old man. 'And who are these two young women? Have you travelled far?' he asked, looking at their weary faces and travel-stained clothes.

'One is Osryth, wife of Aethelred and daughter of Eanfled and Oswy – you may have heard of them – they are from the royal family of Northumbria and the other is Anna, her attendant. We are here to accompany them. We are taking the bones of King Oswald to Bardney. We have travelled from Oswestry. And what is your name?'

'I am known as James the Deacon,' he replied. 'I am old now but in my day I too travelled widely. I have met quite a few churchmen and even royalty during my lifetime,' he added with a wry smile.

Osryth looked surprised and responded, 'But I have heard all about you. Were you not a friend of the priest Paulinus who accompanied my mother to Kent all those years ago?'

There was a short pause and then a look of astonishment. James the Deacon said, 'Well, you must be Eanfled's daughter. I could not quite believe it when the men here just mentioned her. I remember her well. I spend a lot of time here thinking about old times. Yes indeed, Paulinus was a good friend – our ways parted when he accompanied Ethelburga and her son and grandson and Eanfled to Kent. I must be talking about your mother, your grandmother and your uncles – how strange is that? I stayed in York but Lincoln is where I feel most at home. It was Paulinus who was responsible for the building of this great church and it is now rightly called after him, his name but now shortened.' He added, 'It is such a shame that some great storm must have damaged the roof. But at least it now has more light and I love to sit here. I love to see the Roman buildings in this city and imagine the people of times gone by.'

'It is a good building, this church, but not so good in the rain or in the snow, I guess,' said one of the thegns with a smile.

'No indeed,' was the reply. 'It is definitely a church more suited to a warm summer day.'

'I must talk with you,' exclaimed Osryth. 'You must tell me about my mother's childhood. Was it true that my mother was born on a day that someone tried to murder my grandfather Edwin and nearly succeeded? I have heard that the shock of it caused my grandmother to give birth.'

'So I understand; it certainly was a dramatic entry into this world for your mother. I have heard that a servant of Edwin warded off the attack; unfortunately he lost his life for his efforts. And your grandfather was injured. Your mother was born a few hours later. It is said that the shock of the attack must have caused her to give birth early. And I understand that your grandfather was so grateful to survive the attack that your mother became the first child to be born in the kingdom to become a Christian. You certainly have an interesting heritage. I am so pleased to have come across you. Life seems to have come full circle for me,' James the Deacon said to Osryth, still looking at her with amazement.

'And to think that I might not be here had it not been for the actions of that servant,' murmured Osryth in reply. 'You must tell me more about those days. My mother likes to talk of the past but for her it is quite painful to recount some of the traumas she suffered when she was a young girl.'

They stayed awhile all amazed at the coincidence of their meeting. Osryth was pleased that the thegns had encountered someone who knew so much of her family and who could give a very good account of them. In their turn they were amazed at the coincidence of the meeting with the elderly priest and they began to regard Osryth with a new respect.

Later they found a coaching inn in Lincoln for Osryth and Anna to stay. There was not enough room there for the men so they stabled the horses and camped down on the ground next to the carriage which carried Oswald's remains. The thegns had heard of Oswald's magical healing powers. One of them joked, 'Well, our aches and pains should disappear now. This will be a good test of the restoring properties of that casket.' Over a week on horseback and several nights sleeping on the ground had not done their frames any favours. But they looked well and healthy with their faces browned by the sun. And a good night's sleep saw them wake refreshed and good humoured.

And next morning they all set off with fresh spirit. Only a few more miles to go. They were looking forward to a welcome from the monks in Bardney. The thought of this kept their spirits up. They followed the course of the river Witham. The recent rain meant that the river was flowing steadily. They followed along the towpath and they stepped aside where the river had widened and flooded. Progress was slow across the flat landscape; there were brambles to avoid and thick vegetation blocked their way. 'We could do with a scythe,' said one of the thegns. 'I did not think that there would be so many obstacles to encounter.'

It was late afternoon when the community of Bardney was spotted. 'Look to the east of the river,' called Osryth. 'There is a definitely a settlement there – hopefully journey's end.' The group of weary travellers saw a large square settlement in the distance. They found a shallow ford in a narrower part of the river; the horses picked their way gingerly and the thegns waded through groaning inwardly that they had got wet again. And there it was. A cluster of stone buildings, one with a cross on the roof. There was a high stone wall around the buildings and a solid looking wooden gate at the front at the gatehouse. The inhabitants were obviously a practical group of men to have such solid defences. It looked more like a fortress than a monastery

Osryth approached the gate first and rang the bell hanging there. She looked around at her men. They were gently lowering the casket containing the remains of Oswald from the cart. The flag covering it had become even more dilapidated on the journey. It was thin and frayed but the colours were still distinguishable.

Two elderly men dressed in brown monastic habit with tonsured heads opened the gate a few inches. They looked surprised to see the party of thegns and the two women. 'Can we help you?' one of them asked looking suspiciously at the group. Osryth's heart sank. How was she to explain their mission?

'My mother Eanfled sent you a letter I believe a week or so ago. I am now married to Aethelred of Mercia and these are his men. My mother wanted to explain about my visit and her emissary should have travelled here from Whitby.'

'We have had no messengers here,' said one of the monks suspiciously. 'What would the message have been?'

'My father, Oswy of Northumbria, gave the land for this monastery and it was his dearest wish that his brother's remains be buried here. Wherever my uncle is laid to rest his remains are widely reputed to have healing powers. We have the last of his remains in this casket,' Osryth replied, hoping that she sounded more confident than she felt.

The reply came, 'But no one warned us of your visit. I do not know what happened to your mother's messenger but we have not been given any forewarning.' And he added, 'Was your uncle King Oswald of Northumbria? We remember the wars well.'

'Yes, but he was a good man and much blessed. He was a good man of God,' replied Osryth.

'We did not take kindly to being taken over by a foreign power. More recently we supported Wulfhere of Mercia and we do not take kindly to Ecgfrith of Northumbria now being in charge of this area,' said one of the two men and the other nodded in agreement. 'Why should we now venerate your uncle?'

The other man said, 'Is it not normal for some treasure to be buried alongside such a powerful figure?'

Osryth shuddered. She had hoped that this subject would not be mentioned. She thought of the treasure secreted in the ground that she had hoped to retrieve. She realised that admitting that she had lost the hoard may well lead to further problems. 'But we have travelled for days to carry out this mission. And you will find that once you have these relics scores of people will come to Bardney on pilgrimages. My uncle's bones are reputed to have miraculous healing powers,' she insisted.

'We will have to check with the prior later this evening after Compline. But I do not think he will be impressed,' said the more talkative of the two. 'In the meantime we are well guarded and we are not willing for you to breach our defences. How do we know that you are who you say you are?' They turned on their heels and left them where they were. She heard the clang of the bolt as they locked the gate.

This turn of events had not occurred to Osryth. How could she prove that she came in peace and with the best of intentions? She looked around at her surroundings. The thegns did not look impressed.

'Where is this welcome we were promised?' said one of the thegns with a wry look on his face.

Osryth felt mortified. It would be a disaster if having travelled for days she was not allowed to complete her mission. She wished then that she had said more clearly to her mother that a message should be sent to Bardney. She should have listened to her mother and sister and she should have ensured that the monks were happy to receive the remains of her uncle. She could hear dogs barking in the compound. This was not how she had expected to be greeted.

'We will have to put up the tents. It is a warm evening. We will guard our precious casket and perhaps there will be a change of mind in the morning,' said Osryth to her Mercian retinue. 'We can only pray. I have heard that there will be a full moon tonight so at least we will have some light.'

And so it proved.

The tents were put up next to the carriage. Damp clothes were changed and hung to dry. Fresh clothes were found. The rolls of bedding were laid on the ground. Osryth offered to sleep with the casket. She had the company of her attendant, Anna. She did not feel at all fearful. It had been a fine day and the temperature had not dropped. They left the flap of the tent wide open. The moon was bright and the area was flooded with light. A beam caught the edge of the casket and shone so bright that it seemed like daylight. Osryth was unable to settle down or to fall asleep. She could see a number of monks hurrying back to their cells after evening prayer glancing at the illuminated scene. The prior stood at the other side of the gate seemingly lost in wonder. The moonlight continued to beam down in their direction and it reflected off the metal on the casket.

Next morning the gates opened and the prior approached the open tent. He looked as if he too had had an unsettled night. He spoke gently to the two young women now dressed and ready to go on their way. 'I have an apology. I do feel that we have misjudged you. It is unusual to meet a woman travelling on such a mission. And I can see that that casket you carry with you causes miracles to happen.'

Osryth smiled. 'But this is good news. My men will be relieved that we have not come on a fruitless mission. I should have checked that all this was in order before I set out. Does this mean that you are willing to accept this container and that you will look after its precious contents?'

The reply came, 'Well, yes, we will. But first we want to open the casket and wash what bones are there. We will make sure that the remains of King Oswald are treated with due respect.'

And so the monks and Osryth's men gathered around curiously as the casket was opened. Prayers were said and then the white bleached bones were washed gently under running water. Buckets of water had been drawn from the nearby river.

The water that had been used to wash the bones was kept in a separate container. 'This will surely test the healing powers of your uncle,' said one of the monks with a smile on his face.

'And from now on we will keep our gates open and practice the art of hospitality,' the prior added. 'We have had so many attacks from different forces and been under so many different rulers that we have grown isolated and suspicious,' he said in explanation. 'However, we must learn to look at the world outside. We have so many blessings here. Look at the woodland a short distance away and the abundance of wild flowers and butterflies. There is plentiful water and fertile countryside. Our cattle and sheep are well fed and we are self-sufficient with our herbs and vegetables.'

As Osryth looked around she noted the flourishing vegetable patch and the herb garden planted in neat rows. Further afield she could see a herd of cows and dotted around were small flocks of sheep. They had long woollen coats and she could imagine how valuable this must be to them. It was good they lived near to the river. At shearing time the boats could take the wool down the river in both directions, both to the coast and towards Lincoln. He saw her looking and said, 'We do not keep the animals in our compound. That would be cruel. It would be better if there were any raiders that they take those rather than raid our monastery. And I am pleased that you come in peace.'

Oswald's bones were buried in the ground that afternoon and a shrine created. A small wooden structure was created like an altar and the very faded royal emblem was draped over it. A small wooden cross and a candle were placed on the shrine. And another strange occurrence. A young disabled novice washed his hands in the water that had washed Oswald's bones. He stood up straight and stretched. He smiled. 'I feel refreshed and my aching bones no longer feel so much pain.' And he stood up and walked off without limping. This appeared to be a miracle and the monks and Aethelred's men felt humbled by this unexpected event.

Osryth felt as though she knew this place well. Yet,

although she had heard of Lincoln and the province of Lindsey, she had never to her knowledge been to this area before. She longed for a rest and to stay in one place for a period of time. She sighed and said to the prior, 'I am very tired. Could my attendant and I stay in your guest rooms for a week or so? My men can return home and perhaps persuade my husband to follow me here. He would be very impressed with all this.'

Reluctantly the Mercian thegns left her to go on their return journey. What would their king think of this new development? They carried with them a note from Osryth. She wrote in large flowing script asking her husband to come and join her. She described the self-sufficient community in Bardney and the pleasant surroundings. She hoped that he would take the opportunity to spend some time here as a retreat. As she sealed the letter with wax and handed it to the men she said a little prayer to herself. Then she said to the men, 'Please deliver this to Aethelred and say how I am looking forward to showing him round here. He can be assured of a good welcome.'

Her faithful attendant Anna tried to hide her concern but was worried about this new plan. 'How long do you think we will stay here? Will we go back to Tamworth soon?' she asked. Would they forever live in this bleak place? Anna thought to herself. She was hoping to have a lively time at the court at Tamworth and had not anticipated this development. She was beginning to feel homesick for Whitby too; at least her family lived there.

Both women were tired. The gentle routine of the monastic life with the early nights and early mornings suited them both. They slept better than they had for weeks. Gradually the colour returned to their cheeks and they began to look rested and cheerful. And an emissary came with a note from Aethelred. He had written to say that he would be arriving in a couple of days and would travel with his retinue. The overriding emotion Osryth felt was excitement. It was infectious. The monks themselves felt flattered by the attention of royal guests.

In a few days Aethelred arrived accompanied by the very same thegns who had escorted his wife and her attendant. Osryth was delighted to see her husband and Anna seemed equally pleased to see his retinue. Aethelred was intrigued with Lincolnshire, until recently it had belonged to his own kingdom of Mercia. He saw the fertile plains and the well-fed cattle and sheep. He noticed the woodland of lime trees so characteristic of this area. Wood like that would be a very valuable asset. Lime was a very hardy wood often used for constructing shields. It could be used in wood turning, carving and any offcuts would be useful for firewood. The bark was often used to make rope. And the flowers were a valuable source of nourishment for honey bees. No wonder there had been a lot of fighting over this region. He resolved that one day this area would belong to Mercia again. He did not trouble Osryth with this thought. Her brother Ecgfrith had laid claim to it and to reclaim the land may indeed mean another war. And equally Osryth did not trouble Aethelred with the loss of the wedding gift; in any event she was sure that this would be found again. She could not bear the thought of all that glittering jewellery being lost in the ground forever in the middle of some bleak moorland. Who would find it and how long would it take to be found?

Aethelred and Osryth kept their thoughts to themselves. Each day they attended the services in the monastery at Bardney and each day they grew more attached to the settlement there. They tended the animals and collected the vegetables and herbs grown by the monks. They woke up at daybreak and went to sleep as soon as the sun had set. And what a sunset they often saw. It stretched the expanse of the horizon and the fiery colours slowly dying in the sky were memorable. In their spare time they went for long walks along the river and sat on the grass riverbank; sometimes they lay looking up at the wide expanse of blue sky and listened to the sound of the many birds and watched the butterflies and bees as they hovered among the wildflowers. Osryth was so pleased that they had found a place where both of them could be happy. She was very content with her husband and he looked less careworn and more relaxed. She knew that this idyll could not last forever but tried to enjoy it while she could. She and Aethelred talked of their plans for the future and the children they were hoping for and in which royal hall they should live. They talked of the construction of the small church at Atcham and they agreed how welcome it would be if it was named after Bishop Eata from Melrose. They were excited about their life together with its endless possibilities.

The Mercian retinue were getting restive. Why should their king be delayed in this place? The men were more used to fighting. Some of them had been fighting only a year or more ago for Aethelred's brother, Wulfhere, and they were keenly conscious that Ecgfrith of Northumbria, the brother of Osryth, had got the better of them. They could see how smitten Aethelred was with his new bride with her long flowing fair hair and beautiful smile so they held their tongues. Gradually Aethelred, sensing their impatience, allowed some of the retainers to return to Tamworth. 'I will follow you home to Tamworth in due course and I expect you to guard it well in my absence.' He felt safe in this well-guarded fortress of a monastery.

The days passed into weeks and the weeks passed into months. Osryth was hoping that this gentle pace of life would continue; she looked down at her slim figure hoping that she would see a tell-tale swell and that a new life had been created. But there was no sign of this and Osryth became wistful. She would have loved to have a baby and make her husband happy. And in late August Aethelred made the decision to return to Tamworth. Only a few of his retainers remained at Bardney; one of them Edric. An understanding seemed to have arisen between Edric and Anna. Aethelred decided to leave him as the one retainer who would remain at Bardney with the two women.

Aethelred returned with the remainder of his retinue and Osryth felt desolate. She had begun to take Aethelred's company for granted but nothing could match the emptiness that she felt on his departure. It surprised her. She had always been so independent and strong willed. Her love for her husband had grown over the last few months and even Tamworth now had its attraction. She decided to return to the royal hall there in the near future. She would look for the missing treasure on her journey back. She wished she knew the geography of the area better. She might have to inform Anna and Edric of her plans. How else could the wedding gift from Aethelred be found?

In her spare time she drew pictures of what she remembered about the site of the hidden treasure. The drawings were always the same; a large wooded that intersected with another well-used route on the edge of a forest and moorland on a slight incline not far from a small stream. It was quite different from the wide flat plains of Lincolnshire with the beautiful sunsets setting along a wide horizon and even more different from the dramatic hilly landscapes of Bamburgh and Whitby. Surely the location would not be too difficult to identify on her return journey, she thought to herself.

PART 3
AUTUMN

CHAPTER 7
RETURN TO TAMWORTH

'There was a feud one time, begun by your father.'
Line 459 *Beowulf*

The skies took on an ominous grey hue and the evenings were beginning to draw in. In early September preparations were made to return to the royal hall in Tamworth. Osryth and Anna were busy assisting the monks while getting ready for their own return to the Mercian heartlands. The rain had been continuous recently and the plains were in danger of flooding. It was important to return before they were cut off by the water and unable to travel. In the cooler air swifts and swallows which had nested around the monastery swirled spasmodically in the air above them, seeming to contemplate a departure to warmer climes. Every so often a V-shaped formation of geese streaked across the misty landscape.

It was agreed that Osryth and her attendants would be accompanied by four monks from Bardney. The two women and their loyal thegn Edric had gained the respect and affection of the monastic community. They would be missed. Prayers were said for their safe return and they were assured that if ever they wished to return to Bardney that they would be most welcome, as would Aethelred. 'We have enjoyed your company and look forward to you visiting again,' said the prior. 'Do remember us in your prayers and think of the small community here that you have left behind. Hopefully in the warmer weather you will return and your husband too.'

The warm glow that had enveloped Osryth before her wedding had returned. She had never known life to be so happy. She was looking forward to seeing her husband again and perhaps the following year they could again stay in the gentle surroundings of Bardney,

She asked the prior for advice regarding her journey. The reply came, 'The old Roman road, the Fosse Way, will be the best route. Some of it is not much more than a farm track but it runs a straight line. You can return to Tamworth by following Watling Street after the two roads intersect at High Cross.'

At the mention of Watling Street memories of the buried treasure came flooding back to Osryth. She had so wished that she could have brought some treasure with her to honour the memory of her uncle. She wondered whether she would ever come across the spot where it had been deposited. Her memory was becoming hazy as regards the exact location. She was glad that she had sketched some pictures to remind herself. Why does the landscape in Mercia possess so few distinguishing features? she wondered to herself. Wooded roads, small tributaries, gentle inclines and long overgrown tracks intersected with other tracks. It would have been easier to recall the exact location had the landscape been as distinctive and varied as Northumbria or Whitby.

She hoped that the journey back would nudge her memory. They packed the saddlebags with gifts and clothing and food and water bottles and off they started. Jars of honey would be welcome as a gift, she thought. The beehives around Bardney were particularly prolific. Aethelred may well enjoy this touch of luxury. First back to Lincoln and then trudging along the Fosse Way for three days, stopping to stay in small settlements along the route. One was the market town of Leicester. It was a bigger settlement than Tamworth and she saw a bustling marketplace full of chickens and geese and sheep and ox carts bumping along the uneven surface of the streets. The reek of the market place was not a pleasant smell; these settlements could learn a lot from the monastic community, she reflected.

'Oh do we really have to stay here?' she sighed to her companions. 'Could we not just travel a bit further along and perhaps put up a tent when it gets dark?'

'Well there is probably a wayside inn a bit further along,' said one of the monks. And so they trudged on, the women being shaken up and down in the cart as it jolted over the potholes. Osryth reflected on the journey that the religious communities were orderly and clean as far as was possible. She had been pleasantly impressed with both Whitby and Bardney, where there were underground drains and an emphasis on cleanliness. Of course it helped that they were close to rivers, and that each monastery had plenty of land to utilise. Thanks to her father, each abbey had the advantage of many hides of land. The animals could graze on fertile land and were tended by the farm hands; the animals were used for what they could produce; sheep were utilised for their wool and cows for providing milk and cheese and both eventually for meat. Because the abbey community was a large community there was no need to send animals to market.

They were all relieved when they noticed a wayside inn within a short space of time after leaving the busy town. It was time for a quick wash and a deep sleep; they all hoped that their beds were clean but they were really too weary to care very much. Before retiring for the night Osryth said to Anna, 'Well at least it will be a shorter trip than what seemed like the never-ending journey between Oswestry and Bardney. This at least is more direct and journey's end is not too far.'

Anna replied, 'We are certainly very well-travelled now – my life in Whitby was very uneventful before all our adventures on the road.'

Osryth was so impatient to return to Tamworth that she did not pay much attention to the weather or the journey. The weather was nondescript and grey and the evenings were chilly. However, she began to take notice when one of the monks said that they were approaching the crossroads with Watling Street. They reached High Cross. She hoped that this was the same crossroads where she had buried the treasure. And so she looked around eagerly looking for a tell-tale ridge near the crossroads. There was indeed a hill but she was puzzled to see that it seemed steeper than she recalled. And where was the spot where they had deposited the sack? There was no necklace hanging in the tree and no large stakes to mark the spot. Had she made a mistake? Was this the crossroads in question? She wished that her mother and sister were there with her. They would have been able to advise her.

The monks saw her looking around and asked whether she knew the area. She said, 'I am not sure but I would like to have a look around. It will do me good to have some exercise. I get stiff sitting in the one position.'

They were all glad of a break. The road was a straight track but it was a long journey. There had been a Roman settlement at this spot and some of the buildings were still well preserved. Osryth was puzzled. She had not noticed any buildings when she had journeyed with her mother and sister to the crossroads in the bleak moorland that early morning a few months ago. The location of the sack of treasure would remain a mystery. She walked around the picturesque landscape with the monks and tried to recall whether any of it looked familiar.

She did not want to raise the suspicions of her companions and so she tried to memorise what she had seen. She was still reluctant to confide in Anna. The loss of the treasure seemed too momentous to make public and she would like to retrieve it before admitting what had happened. It was puzzling. She was sure that the hoard had been buried at a crossing of the tracks where an old Roman road intersected Watling Street. But was this the right crossroads? She would have to check with her mother and sister and before too long. She did not want to risk the treasure being found by someone else.

They journeyed on and soon there were just a score of miles to complete. The routine of morning prayers and evening prayers continued as it had done throughout the journey. The group would find a sheltered area not far from the road for these brief interludes. Each day they were thankful. The prayers that were recited morning and evening were concise and they seemed very apt. Each day they were grateful they had enough to eat and that they had not met with bandits or roving wild animals. The monks who walked at the head and the back of the procession were glad of this routine. And it gave comfort to Osryth. She felt content that they were on their way to Tamworth. It had only been a short while since Aethelred had gone ahead of her but she realised how much she now depended on his company. An uneasy thought flitted across her mind that she had omitted to send a message in advance about her plans. It would not have been easy to do so from the group of elderly monks in Bardney. Surely Aethelred would not mind if they arrived unexpectedly, Osryth thought to herself. She was looking forward to seeing him. Life was good. She put the thought of the missing treasure to the back of her mind.

As they approached Tamworth Osryth decided to walk for the last few miles. She asked Anna if she was happy to do so also. Both felt this was better than travelling in the makeshift cart that was so uncomfortable on the uneven road. Watling Street was another long straight road but the road surface had deteriorated markedly since Roman times, and the energy expended in walking calmed their excited anticipation at the prospect of reaching the royal hall.

They reached Tamworth in the early evening. It was beginning to get dark and torches had been lit around the hall. It was a dramatic sight and lightened the hearts of those approaching.

Osryth was hoping that Aethelred would come out to greet her. They had been so happy together at Bardney. But there was no sign of him. He must not have realised that their arrival was imminent. She spoke to the guards. They let her and her companion Anna and the monks through the main door and escorted them to the feasting hall.

There they saw Aethelred surrounded by his knights and attended by serving girls enjoying a meal. Aethelred looked surprised to see them. Osryth felt uncomfortable. This was not the welcome she had envisaged. Her face turned hot. 'I am sorry that I did not give you notice of my intentions to return here,' she said to Aethelred. She realised that she should have sent a messenger ahead of her to warn them of her plans. Aethelred made no answer. She was puzzled. She turned to leave the room but Aethelred beckoned her back. It was evident that he had been drinking. This did not appear to have improved his mood. This seemed a different Aethelred from the one whose company she had enjoyed so recently. There was much laughing and joking among the men. The court jester was entertaining the royal party. But Aethelred's face remained set and his eyes were dark and hostile. He pointed to some benches at the wall and told the monks to place them round a table at the far end of the feasting hall. This they did with some concern. They had not seen him act in such a peremptory fashion in the relaxed surroundings of Bardney. He had been helpful and genial when he had been their guest. They were seeing a new side to his character. Osryth and Anna took their seats among their travelling companions. Both felt awkward and would have liked to leave the room. The thegn Edric went to join his colleagues and he too now seemed like a stranger.

Aethelred must have sensed their surprise. He made an effort to be polite and to be a good host and instructed the serving girls to bring them soup from the cauldron over the fire. It was a vegetable broth and served with chunks of bread and cheese. The kitchen staff did not show any sign of recognition towards Osryth and Anna, their faces expressionless and blank as they served the travel-stained and weary travellers. For the travellers it was the first good meal that they had enjoyed since leaving Bardney and they were grateful. But they were all disconcerted at the atmosphere in the royal hall. They felt like intruders and Osryth looked with alarm at her husband.

When they retired for the night she asked him what was wrong. At first he did not reply but then he said in a sharp tone, 'We had cause to look in the strongroom for our swords. We found the key that you had hidden in our bedchamber. I was expecting to see the linen bag containing the marriage gift I gave you in the strongroom. There was no sign of it. Do you know what has happened to it?' he said accusingly.

Osryth felt a rising panic. She did not want to admit that she had lost it or what her plans had been for it. So she told him, 'I gave it for safekeeping to my mother and sister.' This was partly true, she reassured herself.

'But they said that they had no need of any dowry. And why did my soldiers who escorted them home make no mention of it?' he said suspiciously.

'Perhaps they did not realise what it was,' she said. This was dreadful. She had tried to dismiss from her mind the worry about where she had buried the treasure. Here she was making matters worse. It was too late to go back on what she had said.

'Perhaps I should travel back to Whitby and just check that all is in order,' she said. 'I need to reassure myself that everything is where it should be. And after all, as you know the gift you gave me became my property on marriage and I should not have to make explanation to you,' she said defiantly.

'But as you know that gift was in the hope that we have a family and I gave it to you in case anything happens to me. Not that you would care,' he added angrily, his voice raised.

'But how can you say that? You must know how much I care for you,' she replied.

He said sarcastically, 'That is why you went away for weeks after our marriage only to summon me to Lincolnshire which is now, just to make matters worse, in your family's hands and no longer belongs to Mercia. Was it just to remind me of the wars my brother waged with your brother in the last few years? Well, if so, it certainly brought back all those recent memories'

'But I thought we were happy together. And I thought that you liked Bardney,' was the reply.

'I did find it a pleasant change, I have to admit, but you seem to forget that I am the king of Mercia and I cannot escape to a rural idyll for months on end, however much I may want to,' he retorted.

And then both of them were upset. Osryth asked if anything else was amiss. She was told that there was trouble brewing in Kent. Two young princes, both related to him and one even bearing the same name as him, Aethelred, had been murdered in the near past. Bishop Putta of Rochester had recently brought his choir to Lichfield. He had relayed these dreadful events. Hlothhere, the King of Kent, was getting overconfident and was becoming a threat to Surrey, a Mercian area. Aethelred was gathering together his troops. He did not want his kingdom to shrink even further. He needed the swords for his foray to Kent.

'But why Kent?' Osryth asked. 'Surely you know that my mother comes from Kent and Hlothhere is her cousin. My mother's family built the first stone church in Lyminge near the coast.'

'Oh, I dare say I would not venture that far. However, Putta has come from Rochester and he has told me of the great riches in the church and castle there. If we have nothing left here in the way of valuables the riches may as well come to the Mercians, who as you know until recently ruled Kent. And that might deter King Hlothhere from invading Surrey and taking even more territory from us. He is living up to his name "the looter"!

'But surely if you raid his monasteries and churches are you not in danger of becoming the same as him? And as a Christian should you not treat churches wherever they are with more respect?' Osryth said.

Aethelred looked at her sharply. 'Treasure means power. The Church should be able to exist on its own merits. It should not need gold and silver and baubles,' he replied, and added, 'But kingdoms are quite fragile and I do not want to go down in history as a weak king who can be taken for a fool. We need to have reserves of gold and jewellery.' She did not like to contradict him and knew what he was saying was based on fact, but she was alarmed at his talk of war. This was not how she had anticipated her homecoming.

Osryth felt a great weariness. She had hoped to tell him that she was an expectant mother but she knew this was not so. Each month she had been disappointed. She knew that he loved children; she had seen how he had enjoyed the company of their nieces and nephews. What would happen if she never bore his children? she wondered. Would she be cast off? At least there was one consolation. She was still able to travel easily, even though she longed for a more settled life. So she said again more firmly, 'Well, I will travel to Whitby in a week or so just to see everything is in order there. And then I would like to come back to Tamworth and we must not be suspicious of one another. We know that we can be happy.' His brow furrowed and he looked unhappy. He shrugged his shoulders. This was not promising. She resolved to leave the next morning.

CHAPTER 8
RETURN TO WHITBY

'all of us with souls, earth-dwellers
and children of men, must make our way
to a destination already ordained
where the body, after the banqueting,
sleeps on its deathbed.' **Lines 1003-1007** *Beowulf*

Early next morning Osryth gathered up her clothes. She told Anna to pack her belongings. They were neither of them comfortable in this atmosphere. Anna had not liked to ask Osryth about the reason for the hostile reception.

'Are you not going to say goodbye to your husband?' Anna asked in surprise.

'No, he is out hunting and I do not expect he will be back for hours. He will have to make do with a note. We need an early start for our journey,' replied Osryth coolly.

It was very different from the comfortable atmosphere in Bardney where they had both felt appreciated particularly in recent weeks. Anna was puzzled. What on earth could have caused such a rift between the married couple? she wondered. And Edric was none the wiser. Aethelred had obviously not confided in him. Visiting their families in Whitby was preferable to this scenario despite the distances involved.

'I have upset Aethelred without meaning to,' Osryth said to Anna. She was still reluctant to discuss the details of the loss of the buried treasure with her. She did not know who to trust and even Edric may betray any confidences. 'We will travel to Whitby to visit our families. You must miss your family as much as I miss mine. There is no need to forewarn them – we can both be sure of a welcome in Whitby whether they know about our journey or not,' she added, thinking regretfully of her husband's reaction to their unexpected arrival.

There would not be so much of an entourage as she had been given on her journey to Oswestry. Edric would be the only thegn to guard them. To her surprise the monks from Bardney who had accompanied them to Tamworth asked to visit Whitby too. Their prior had already approved an extended break. She felt moved by their insistence. She was beginning to feel as though she did not belong anywhere. This gave her some reassurance. The monks welcomed the opportunity to visit the monastery in Whitby. They were enjoying a change of routine. The winter months could seem very long in the Lincolnshire plains and they were interested to see the renowned Whitby Abbey, famous after the Synod of Whitby a decade earlier. They would have to ask permission of Abbess Hilda on their arrival. They were confident that she would approve their visit. From Whitby the monks from Bardney could return directly to their monastery, choosing the most convenient way to travel.

So again the horse and cart were prepared. This would be a long journey taking at least a week with the monks walking most of the time. Tents were put in the cart. Despite the coolness in the weather there may not always be an inn by the roadside for a night's rest. They seemed so free and happy not only to walk but also to put up with the privations of accommodation that it lightened the mood of both Osryth and Anna. Osryth felt as though she were escaping. She had only returned to the royal hall the evening before but she realised that it was impossible to stay longer in the company of her husband while he was in this dark mood. It was the first time that she had seen this side of his character. She began to wonder about the wisdom of marrying the son of her father's long-time enemy. Her husband was obviously not happy either. She had not anticipated his displeasure about the loss of the treasure. She wished that she had told him the entire truth. It was difficult to maintain the half-truth she had blurted out. Aethelred had gone out with his thegns early in the morning to hunt deer and she was glad that she could not say her farewell to him. She left a note in her flowing script explaining what she was doing.

She sighed a deep sigh when she realised that the route planned to Whitby was via Alfreton and York. She would not be retracing her steps along Watling Street. So there was no chance of looking for that elusive treasure on this journey. However, she could ask her mother and sister for advice and perhaps one of them at least could accompany her on her return and help her find the spot where they had buried the hoard. The stakes they had left there and the glittering necklace in the branches of the tree above would guide them to the right place. There was still hope that the morning gift could be retrieved.

And so the procession wound its way along country tracks towards Alfreton. The routine had become familiar. The horse pulling the cart, Edric on horseback with his sword at the ready keeping a look out for bandits and wild animals, two monks with crosses at the front of the procession and two with similar brown robes and crosses at the back. The two at the back were a genial pair with a joke ready when needed to lighten their spirits. They were now like friends. All were at ease with each other and only spoke when they needed to. It was a comfortable silence. The two at the front were the monks who had greeted them so suspiciously when they had arrived at Bardney. They were enjoying their adventure and seemed to have become more protective. Osryth suspected that they felt a little sorry for her after the brusque reception at Tamworth.

The leaves on the trees were turning russet and the winds were getting chilly. The monks were glad of their long robes which kept them warm. Osryth gathered her cloak around her and covered her head. She no longer had the sense of anticipation and excitement that she had experienced on her journey to Bardney. She was more reflective. She wanted to savour the freedom of travel. She reflected on her marriage. She knew that Aethelred was a good man and had converted to Christianity. And his affection had been so steady during their courtship and during the first few weeks of marriage. Why should the loss of the treasure have made such a difference to him? After all, she was sure that it had originally belonged to her family. Would they always be suspicious of one another? If only she could be blessed with a child this might well change.

She thought of her late father Oswy and sighed. He had been close to his daughter Osryth. She was often told by her father how she reminded him of his brother Oswald with her tall stature and golden hair and fine features. Was this why she had been so anxious to do what her father had wanted as regards Oswald's remains? she wondered. And even on Oswy's deathbed he had repeated his wish that Bardney should be his brother Oswald's final resting place, and how he wished he had kept some of the treasure to honour him at his place of burial. How could she have done otherwise? she thought.

And so the journey continued. The young attendant Anna was looking forward to welcoming Edric to Whitby. The two seemed engrossed in each other's company. They kept close to one another and sat together in the firelight in the evenings. Some evenings they had to sleep under the makeshift canopies that they kept in the cart. None of them were far apart but

Anna and Edric were always close to each other. And in the daytime they moved around as if in a bit of a dream. They were a handsome pair with their dark hair and fresh complexions. Perhaps there was some Celtic background there, Osryth wondered. Edric was quiet and Anna was the outgoing character. They seemed very well suited. Osryth hoped that their relationship would progress better than her own relationship with her husband. Perhaps she and Aethelred were too similar; she reflected on how strong willed they both were. What a shame that everything between them had suddenly become so fraught, she thought, sometimes close to tears. She felt that she was less important in Aethelred's eyes than the treasure she had been given.

The small group continued on their way. After Alfreton they were aiming to reach York in a couple of days. Osryth had heard much about York. She knew that a timber church, the minster, had been built especially for the occasion of the christening of her grandfather, King Edwin. It had then been rebuilt in stone by her uncle Oswald and more recently the roof repaired and glass added thanks to Wilfred, the priest of high status. Wilfred had been a familiar figure in the court at Bamburgh and Osryth could recall him telling her father about the progress of the renovations. She looked forward to seeing the church.

When they approached York in the early evening they saw a dramatic spectacle. Torches with blazing flames were being carried around the walls. Scores of men, women and children were dressed in long robes and walking towards the green in front of the minster. 'It must be a mystery play,' said one of the monks. 'We are so fortunate to see this.' And they spent the next two hours watching dramatic scenes re-enacted from the Bible. There was a musical accompaniment: drums, flutes and a harp in the background. How magical it all sounded.

The next morning after resting in a coaching inn they were all free to explore York. They could wander along the narrow criss-crossed streets, many of which were cobbled and uneven underfoot. They looked up at the walls around the city which dated back to Roman times. And they saw the small boats which were moored at the harbour on the side of the wide river. This was by far the most exciting place they had visited. They were not surprised that the priest Wilfred had spoken so warmly of York to Osryth's parents. It was a vibrant community. There was a large marketplace selling fruit and vegetables and leather goods as well as crafts of all sorts. 'Look, Anna, I wish we had this choice of goods in Whitby. What amazing craftsmen they have here,' Osryth called out excitedly.

Nearby, the minster was both well constructed and well placed in the city close to both the walls and the river. Osryth wished that she could draw an illustration of it for Hilda. Even if she had had the drawing materials she wondered whether she could do it justice. She had heard that Hilda had been christened in the minster at the same time as Osryth's grandfather, Edwin. Hilda had been thirteen at the time. Hilda was Edwin's niece and a cousin of Osryth's mother Eanfled. Eanfled's own views of York were tinged with sadness at the memories of the horror of her father Edwin's death. But Hilda do doubt would have been interested to visit York again had her health allowed this. Since the conversion of that area to Christianity all those years ago the country was reputed to be a much safer place to visit and travel around. Whatever one's views it was certain that the conversion of the people led to a more civilised community, Osryth reflected.

As they eventually departed from York, Osryth's travelling companions commented on how far she had travelled across the country since her marriage.

'And before it. I seem impelled to see the whole of the country – I must be a restless soul. I should have drawn a map. I only wish my geography was better,' she said with a wry smile. 'There seems to be a common theme to all of this. Firstly to show Aethelred my beautiful Northumbria and secondly to carry out the mission of burying the remains of my uncle in a shrine at Bardney. I am amazed that we have not had any more mishaps. I have not counted the distance - perhaps just as well,' she added, 'Although I was not anticipating this particular journey I am thoroughly enjoying it. And what memories I shall have. But one day I do wish to be settled and stay in just one place.'

'You never know, perhaps you will join us in Bardney and perhaps Aethelred too. You both seemed so happy there. And we will have the healing power of Oswald's relics,' said one of the monks.

Osryth smiled. The prospect seemed very attractive. If she moved to Bardney there would be no more talking of warmongering or tension with other kingdoms. Aethelred had been so happy and content in the Lincolnshire countryside. She could learn many skills from the monks. She could be taught how to illustrate manuscripts and study animal husbandry and how to become self-sufficient by growing crops. She could be shown how to play a musical instrument, perhaps a harp with its rippling sound that could move one so easily to tears. She could learn Latin. She could live a simple life like her mother and sister. They would be not too far distant from one another. Tamworth seemed like another world. And the grim reality of living there had struck her forcibly on her brief recent visit. Even if Aethelred had been more welcoming recently at his royal hall she could not get away from the feeling that she was in a strange land there far from her family. The Mercian thegns seemed suspicious of her and she wondered if she would ever be properly accepted by them. The one exception was the loyal thegn, Edric. Osryth could see that he was becoming inseparable from Anna. This was bound to affect his views and foster a sense of loyalty. It would not surprise her in the least if they, Edric and Anna, eventually got married. Perhaps then Edric would feel equally at home in Northumbria as in Mercia. He may end up having split loyalties like her. She hoped that his life and that of Anna's would be more straightforward than her own.

'I would like to visit the priory at Lastingham. It is not far from Whitby,' declared Osryth. 'My cousin Ethelwald was responsible for its foundation and even though the brothers Cedd and Chad who built it are both departed from this life I understand that Ethelwald, the son of Oswald, is now there as a monk. I hear that he is much more attached to this wooden building built by Cedd than he ever was to his kingdom of Deira.'

And so after York they made the journey to Whitby. Osryth was full of mixed emotions. She was no longer the confident young woman who was certain that her future would be exciting and carefree. She had begun to doubt herself and the wisdom of her actions. Every time that the niggling doubts crept into her mind she tried to breathe more easily. Life on earth was so short and she had to make the best of it. She knew she was more fortunate than many of the women around her. Their lives seemed quite limited. Growing vegetables, cooking and washing and bearing children, many of whom died quite young, seemed to be their lot. At the thought of children she again felt wistful and wished there was good news to impart to her mother and sister. It seemed as though her mother would never know the joys of grandchildren. There was no sign of

Osryth herself becoming pregnant, her brother Ecgfrith did not yet have any children despite being married for the second time and her sister Aelfflaed was a nun. Her youngest brother, Aelfwine, was only in his mid-teens but by all accounts was growing into a fine youth. Still they were all relatively young, she reflected. And having children did not necessarily mean that the offspring would be loyal. There had been tensions between her elder half-brother Alchfrid and their father, Oswy, before Alchfrid's disappearance. They had disagreed about whether the practices of the Roman church should take precedence over that of the Celtic church. What a petty disagreement in the larger scale of things Osryth reflected. And yet the subject was so important to so many people whichever side they had backed. It was a shame that Alchfrid had disappeared before any proper reconciliation. The plague had decimated many in the population.

Oswald's son, Ethelwald, had fought with Penda against Oswy, his father's brother. And even if he had stood aside at the last moment to allow Oswy to win the battle, it seemed that he had very mixed loyalties. Osryth herself did hope that there would be an obvious successor after Aethelred, who would unite the kingdoms of Northumbria and Mercia. Too long the young men of both kingdoms had fought in battles and been killed or badly wounded. And some of them had dropped out of the fight for whatever reason.

When they reached Lastingham, a wooden monastery

147

on the way to Whitby, they stopped. Cedd had built the small priory under the guidance of Ethelwald. The location was beautiful, set as it was in the undulating and wild landscape. It was a shame that Cedd, like so many, had died of the plague after the Synod of Whitby and his brother Chad had taken over. Now in turn he had died. Osryth wished to see her cousin but Ethelwald could not be prevailed upon to meet them. On their departure after a good meal in the refectory Osryth caught a glimpse of a grizzled grey-haired monk. He bore more than a passing resemblance to Oswy, who would have been his uncle. Their eyes met briefly and then the monk averted his gaze. She was convinced that it was Ethelwald. What a shame, she thought, that the troubles of the past still enveloped him. So much for family ties. She wondered whether he had heard of her arrival or whether he recognised her; maybe she was mistaken but in their family many similarities seemed to have travelled along an extended family tree. Many of the cousins and second cousins resembled each other. She would have liked to have told Ethelwald about Bardney and her mission to honour the remains of his father's body. Perhaps he had heard and was not too pleased. She did not know what to make of the averted gaze. Maybe it was that he preferred solitude and was not used to the company of women. Or maybe she was mistaken about the resemblance.

The journey progressed further toward their destination. The days as well as the evenings were getting colder. Trees became more clearly silhouetted against the sky as leaves of varying shades of red and yellow fluttered down covering the paths. Sounds were muffled by the dense matting of leaves and every now and then the pungent smell of wood smoke filled the air. Small settlements were passed on the route.

Osryth was looking forward to reaching the abbey at Whitby. It was strange to think that only six months had passed since she and Aethelred paid their first visit there. It seemed an age away. So much had happened, the betrothal and the wedding, the journey to Oswestry and Bardney and here she was back on the road again. But she could not wait to see her mother and sister and before long the travellers were climbing up the long flight of steps to Whitby Abbey. The monks from Bardney were looking around with interest. The landscape could not have been more different from the flat marshy plains of Lincolnshire. But once they reached the abbey they felt on familiar territory. There was the stone church on the headland and, close by, the rectangle of wooden buildings, the workshops, the refectory, the guest rooms and outbuildings for the animals.

The travellers went to see Hilda, who was resting. It was important to get the permission of the abbess before staying in the abbey. This was part of the monastic discipline. Osryth was shocked to see Hilda. She had aged considerably since Osryth had last seen her. Osryth knew that Hilda's health was declining,

Osryth's mother, who was tending to Hilda, looked as well as ever and Aelfflaed glided quietly into the room, delighted to see her sister and the new guests. Despite her worn appearance Hilda was very welcoming to her visitors. She asked Eanfled and Aelfflaed to tell the cooks to prepare a feast in their honour. There was an excited atmosphere around the community. And for the first time for months Osryth laughed and joked with her sister and felt as though the burdens of the recent months had been shaken off. Their pet dog jumped up with excitement at the arrival of a familiar face. The thought of the buried treasure was pushed to the back of Osryth's mind. Mingled odours of roasted chickens and smoked bacon and vegetables drifted through the old walls of the abbey. She realised how hungry she was after all the days on the road.

Edric was shown around the family farm where Anna had been brought up. Her parents were surprised and pleased to show her round with the handsome young Mercian. They had not anticipated this friendship. They hoped that this would not mean Anna leaving permanently to live in Mercia. And they had hardly any time for this thought to cross their mind when Edric took Anna's father aside and asked if he would give Edric permission to marry Anna. 'You must treat her well,' said Anna's father, 'She is very precious to us and we do not want her to change.'

Edric said that he wished he himself had more of a

family. He was an only child. His father had been killed a few years previously in battle and his mother died a year later of an illness. He had been brought up in the royal hall of Tamworth.' I will enjoy having a new family, and of course I will treat her well. We are sure that we will both be happy. And I will always look after her. If she wants to live near you in Whitby we will try to do that. I want to be there with her. Now our kingdoms are more united I do not think there should be any problems with that. And I feel very honoured that Aethelred of Mercia has entrusted me with not only the care of Anna but also the protection of his wife, Osryth.'

Anna's father shook Edric by the hand. He was almost overcome with emotion. It was a proud moment for him. He was happy to agree that Edric and Anna could get married and so the young couple went to tell Osryth. They wanted her to be the first person to know about this new development. They regarded her like part of their family; the travels had brought them all closer together. Osryth was delighted to hear their news but could not help feeling a small pang of jealousy. Their life was ahead of them with no secrets such as the one she guarded.

She said briskly, 'We must celebrate this good news. I did anticipate that this might happen. We will have a feast tomorrow in your honour and toasts can be given and you can work out where you would like to be married. I am sure that you would be very welcome to have a wedding here in the abbey. You could not ask for a more appropriate location.'

And so the next day the whole party gathered together in the refectory. The monks from Bardney introduced themselves and one of them said a prayer. They all sat down. Then Edric took Anna to the front of the hall, knelt down in front of her and offered her a small filigree ring. It had been his mother's ring and he had kept it safe and hidden all this time. Anna laughed.

'Well, I can't possibly refuse now can I? A gold ring indeed! I do not know how you managed to keep this a secret from me.' And she accepted the ring and put it on the fourth finger of her left hand with a flourish.

At the mention of the words 'secret' and 'gold' Osryth went pale. She had yet to confide in her mother and sister about the loss of the treasure. They must think that she had moved it safely to Bardney. But nothing of the sort. There it was lying forgotten in the ground somewhere a few miles from Tamworth. It was the quantity of items that upset Osryth. Had it been just a few gold items their loss would not have seemed so momentous. She shook her head wondering why she had made life so complicated for herself. And why had she involved her mother and her sister in her actions. They had only had a quick glimpse of the contents of the linen bag. They would not have even realised the value of what they were hiding in the ground.

After the engagement ceremony she sought her mother and sister out. Osryth felt tearful. She was tired after her long journey and wondered why she put herself through such a punishing schedule. She felt feverish and Eanfled and Aelfflaed were alarmed to see her looking so unwell. Perhaps she had caught a fever. 'Osryth, you must rest. We will bring you some warm milk and honey. Please go straight to your room and we can attend to you there.'

She looked very different from when they had last seen her. In Tamworth she had been a radiant bride and everything seemed to be going her way. What had happened in the meanwhile? She had aged at least ten years and she looked less sure of herself. She went to her room and lay on her bed. Eanfled followed her. 'Has Aethelred been unkind to you?' asked her mother.

She replied, 'No, not exactly.'

'Then what is the problem?' her mother persisted.

Osryth said slowly, 'He has discovered that his wedding gift to me is missing and he is not at all happy about it.'

'But surely it was yours to keep. Have you explained about dedicating it to your uncle at Bardney?' said Eanfled

Osryth's lips trembled.

'What on earth is the matter?' asked her mother. 'This is not like you. You look really troubled.'

Tears welled up in Osryth's eyes. She bit her lip to try to regain some control over her emotions. However, it was good to have someone to confide in. 'Everything has turned out such a disaster. I do not know why I suggested burying the treasure. I could not find where we left it when I looked for it again. I am not even sure that on all my journeying we actually went near it. There are so few landmarks in the Mercian landscape and it all looks very similar to me. So it is in the middle of some bleak moorland in Mercia and no one is any the wiser or happier. The monks in Bardney were disappointed that I did not bring treasure when I took the remains of Oswald and now Aethelred thinks I have given it all to you. He is so angry and really upset and now he is talking about invading Kent.'

'Why on earth would he do that? You have only been married for just over six months. And does he not know of my connections with Kent?' said Eanfled.

'He must have his reasons,' said Osryth. 'I rather suspect that one of his main objectives is to replace the treasure he has lost.'

She closed her eyes, drifting off to sleep and her mother sat on the bed looking at her pale but still beautiful daughter. Was this the same confident, adventurous young woman who she had seen at the abbey in April? The radiance had disappeared and her face had lost its bloom. Perhaps this was just the effect of travelling over a long period of time. But it did not bode well for the marriage. Eanfled wondered whether she was wise to have agreed to her daughter's wedding to Aethelred. If only Osryth could have married someone from Northumbria that surely would not have caused so many problems. She remembered the battles of times past. Penda, the father of Aethelred, had always been their enemy. She had never got over the horror of the death of her father Edwin and brothers all those years ago. And her hasty retreat to Kent as a young girl with her mother and priest and two younger brothers was still a vivid memory. Even in Kent they had felt vulnerable and sent the two younger brothers to France to keep them safe; sadly both brothers had died there of ill health. And since her marriage there had been no peace. Penda had been an angry threat in the background for many years

Eanfled had to shake herself to return to the present; now the immediate priority for Eanfled was to return her daughter to full health. A rest in Whitby and the companionship of her family for a while should help Osryth to recuperate. Her figure was still as slim as ever, perhaps too thin. Eanfled would have liked to have seen signs of a future generation. Perhaps it was not her lot in life to become a grandparent, she reflected sadly.

For the next few days Osryth rested in bed. Gradually she felt stronger and less tearful. Her sister Aelfflaed visited her and gently asked her if she could do anything to help. Osryth explained that Aethelred had not been happy that she had left him for several weeks and that he was angry now he realised that the treasure was missing.

'That should not be a problem,' replied Aelfflaed. 'I will return with you and we will find the treasure again. And surely your husband realises it is quite usual for the remains of a royal relative to be taken to a place of their family's choosing. If it helps I would like to find the remains of our grandfather Edwin and bring them back here from their resting place where they were laid after the Battle of Hatfield Chase. Our mother has often spoken of this. If Aethelred realises that is what I am doing, that your own sister is doing very much the same as what you have done, perhaps he will realise that it is our custom to look after the dead with proper respect. We are not strange in that; remember how we heard about Cadfan, the father of Cadwallon, was buried with such pomp and ceremony in North Wales.'

Osryth smiled a wan smile. 'You have a solution for everything. I do not know whether this will work but I am sure Mother would be pleased.'

'She would be delighted. She often speaks with regret about her father's body still lying near the battlefield. It is not so arduous a journey as the one that you have undertaken. But it will also fulfil a long-held wish by our family that we stay close to each other both in life and death,' replied her sister.

'I feel so far away from you all when I am in Mercia. I feel like a foreigner and sometimes the hostile way that some of the people in the royal court look at me I think that they regard me as such. I think that is part of the reason why I am so glad to travel,' said Osryth sadly.

'But your wedding in Tamworth was so joyful. And I thought that you said that you and Aethelred both really enjoyed life together in Bardney,' replied Aelfflaed.

'Oh, we did. It was the happiest I have been since my marriage. But of course Aethelred cannot just retreat from his life as a king. He is a good man but he has affairs of state to consider. He does not want to lose territory even if is as far away to the south,' replied Osryth, realising that she was repeating Aethelred's words to her and that she was trying to justify the strains in her marriage.

'Well, it can do no harm if I travel to Hatfield Chase near Doncaster to retrieve the remains of our grandfather. It will give you time to recuperate. And I will write to Aethelred saying that you are unwell and that we are nursing you back to full health. And in the meantime we have to arrange the wedding of your attendant, Anna, with your thegn, Edric, who has served you so loyally and kept you safe in your travels,' said Aelfflaed.

'Could you also mention the happy news of the wedding of Anna and Edric to Aethelred in your letter to him? He will be pleased about that, I am sure,' replied Osryth.

Aelfflaed went to the scriptorium and wrote a letter to Aethelred explaining that her sister was unwell and that she needed time to recuperate. She mentioned that she herself was going on a mission to retrieve the remains of her grandfather Edwin. She explained that it was not a long journey but was a mission that had long been hoped for in particular by her mother. In the meantime Osryth would be well looked after by her mother and would be helped by the fresh sea air and also by the good food served in the abbey. She added a postscript that Edric and Anna would marry in a month's time in Whitby and that Aethelred was most welcome to attend. She read the letter over and smiled. No one could take exception to any of that, she thought to herself. She sealed the letter with wax and handed it to one of the monks from Whitby to take on a delegation to Aethelred. It needed to be delivered as soon as possible, she told him.

The monk in question, Osbert, was attended by two other monks from Whitby. They looked forward to travelling to an area new to them. Tamworth was a long journey but this was a privilege. The monks were chosen for their relative youth and stamina. The horses that they would use were groomed and new horseshoes made for them in the smithy situated within the confines of the monastic community. The sparks flew upwards as the blacksmith did his work, the horses waiting patiently nearby until they were shod and considered fit to undertake a long journey.

The monks were waved off by Osryth and her mother Eanfled. They were given directions to travel via York, Doncaster and Sutton-in-Ashfield. They had enjoyed the camaraderie with the monks from Bardney and looked forward to their turn travelling across the country. They were not fearful. They knew that the journey would take several days. They relished the prospect of travelling through the centre of the country and the new sights they would see.

Aelfflaed accompanied the monks as far as Doncaster. It was her turn to carry out a mission. She was spurred on not only by the courage of her sister but also by the thought that she might help Osryth's troubled marriage by carrying out a similar mission. She was searching for the remains of her long-dead grandfather, Edwin, who had been buried there after the Battle of Hatfield Chase. He had been defeated and killed by the combined forces of Penda and Cadwallon. After many enquiries, a very elderly woman had been found who could point her to the spot where his body was laid to rest. This was just as well, otherwise her mission could have been a complete failure. They were still in their own kingdom of Northumbria so no permission was needed to carry out the search.

After the retrieving of a winding sheet, and its contents from the shallow grave were identified, a trusted retainer of Aelfflaed put the remains, wrapped in old linen, in their cart. Edwin's body had been buried on his own, slightly apart from the main cemetery, a fact that indicated that he was of high status. A small cross had been found in the grave, a fact that reassured them that this was indeed the skeleton of Edwin, buried over forty years previously. His skull was separate from the rest of his body. Again this was good proof that this was the correct grave. Aelfflaed had heard that her grandfather had been beheaded after battle and his head put on a stake; she was glad that after that ignominious end that her grandfather's remains could be buried again with proper respect.

She shuddered at the thought of the brutal death of her grandfather. His death seemed far removed from the peaceful life in the monastery at Whitby. But no wonder that her mother was always fearful. What a shock it must have been for her mother and grandmother to witness such tragedy, thought Aelfflaed. No wonder she and her mother had to retreat to Kent all those years ago with their priest Paulinus. And it had given her something in common with her husband, Oswy, whose brother's death had also been so brutal. What was it about her family? she wondered. There seemed no end to the warfare and early deaths they had endured. Perhaps, she reflected sadly, that was the penalty for living in a divided country in these troubled times. Seven provinces and none of the rulers secure in their kingdoms.

The party said a short prayer and then Aelfflaed and her companions made the journey back to Whitby at a gentle pace. Eanfled would be very pleased that the bones of her father had been retrieved. They knew that to her it was very important that her family should stay together whether in life or death. And as they had thought Eanfled was indeed delighted on their return. She had embroidered a white cloth with gold thread in the shape of a cross to be used as a fresh winding sheet. She came out to greet them as they approached with the cart trailing behind with its valuable load. Later that day.

as planned, a service was held at the abbey. The remains of Edwin were placed in a grave close to the abbey and a funeral ceremony was held to commemorate this solemn occasion. Plenty of tears were shed, but some of the tears arose from relief that at long last the body of Edwin had been brought home.

In the meantime, the monks from Whitby were continuing their journey towards Tamworth. Osbert, the lead monk, kept the sealed letter of Aelfflaed close to him. He knew how important it was to deliver it safely. He had noticed how unwell Osryth had appeared before they had left for Mercia; he considered it only fair that her husband Aethelred should know as soon as possible.

CHAPTER 9
A ROYAL DISAGREEMENT

'... Then whoever wants to
may go bravely to mead, when morning light,
scarfed in sun-dazzle, shines forth from the south
and brings another daybreak to the world.'
Lines 603-606 *Beowulf*

Aethelred was in the courtyard of his royal hall in
Tamworth when the three monks from Whitby arrived.
It was midday and a group of his soldiers were training
in the courtyard. One of his guards approached him and
informed him that there were emissaries from Whitby
waiting at the front gate.

Aethelred was surprised. He had had time to regret
his coolness towards Osryth. Their marriage had started
out with so much promise. He looked back at their
sojourn in Bardney as the happiest time of his life. What
a shame that he was now king, he sometimes reflected.
His life was mapped out now in a way that he had
never expected. He had not expected either the violent
death of his eldest half-brother, Paeda, nor the death of
his elder brother Wulfhere. He had not been trained in
kingship and sometimes he looked back on his father
Penda's warlike exploits with alarm. His conversion to

Christianity had given him some self-awareness. He hoped that he would not turn out to be as ruthless as his father. But neither did he wish to appear feeble; these were violent days and there were many who would exploit any weakness.

He went to meet the visitors flanked by two of his soldiers. He greeted the group of monks politely and invited them in. They went through the vast hall into an anteroom. With a flourish Osbert handed over the letter that Aelfflaed had written. Aethelred read it in front of them. He was surprised that Osryth herself had not written. He asked them why she had not written a letter herself.

'She is not well at present,' said the lead monk to him. Aethelred did not reply to that. He suspected that Osryth had not forgiven him for asking where she had taken the wedding gift of treasure that he had given her. Surely it had been reasonable of him to challenge her about that.

He said to the monks, 'My wife seems to feel that her treasure is safer in Whitby than here. You must have a very secure strongroom in the abbey.'

The monks looked puzzled. 'Sire, we do not wish to be rude but we know nothing of any treasure. We do not have a strongroom in the abbey. Apart from our manuscripts and our gold thread and our paints we do not have much of any value. What makes you think we have any treasure?'

Aethelred did not answer. He read the letter again.

'What is this about Edric getting married?' he asked. 'Why has he not asked for my permission? After all he is one of my thegns and much as I think Anna and he are well suited it would have been better had he approached me first.'

Osbert replied, 'Well perhaps he meant to ask you. It is a shame that Tamworth and Whitby are so far apart. I do believe that he thought that he should first ask Anna's father. Edric told us he had lost his own parents and perhaps he overlooked asking you. They are busy planning the wedding in Whitby and very much hope that you will honour the occasion by your attendance.'

Aethelred looked at the monk suspiciously. Was he being facetious? With all the problems in the southern kingdoms of the country Aethelred considered that it was unlikely that he would have the time or inclination to go to a wedding on the other side of the country. In any event his security may be in jeopardy. He remembered with a shudder the death of Paeda, his oldest brother. It had happened in Northumbria. It was said that Osryth's oldest half-sister, Paeda's wife, was involved in some way with the murder of Paeda. Who knows what fate might await him if he was surrounded by the family of Oswy.

He read again the section of the letter about retrieving the bones of Edwin. This was all ridiculous, he thought to himself. It was all based on pagan customs and rituals. His own father's body lay where it had fallen during the Battle of the Winwaed near the great river that had taken his life. It seemed better and more seemly thus, he thought to himself. Why on earth would one want to travel around the country chasing after bones? And perhaps not even be sure that they were the actual bones that were sought.

He was determined not to voice his suspicions to the monks. He did not want to criticise his wife or her family in front of his soldiers or in front of strangers. After all they were only emissaries. And they had a long journey and must need refreshment. So he beckoned to his serving girls to prepare a meal for his visitors. The monks were glad of a rest from travelling and looked forward to their first warm meal for a week. Soon the wafts of ham and leek soup drifted through from the kitchen. The visitors sat round a trestle table and were glad of his hospitality. The ale that was served quenched their thirst. The bread and soup was very welcome. 'This should keep us going for some time,' one of them said aloud.

Later they were given sleeping quarters in the monastery nearby. However, much to their surprise Aethelred did not write a letter to Whitby in return. When he summoned the monks next morning to his presence he said coolly that he hoped that they would pass on his message that he had no plans to travel to Whitby for the wedding of his thegn but he wished the young couple well. He also said, 'I hope that Osryth will soon be well enough to rejoin me in Tamworth. She must bear in mind that in the next month or two I will be travelling to Kent and she must forgive me if I am away when she returns.' He then said that there was no need for this to be written down. He trusted them to summarise what he had said.

It was then time for the three monks to retrace their steps to Whitby. They were puzzled as to why Aethelred had been so distant. As messengers they were not offered armed protection. His thegns gave them directions. The monks had their long knives to ward off any wolves or brigands and they felt confident enough to vary their route. They believed the crosses which they carried would keep them safe. This time the journey would take them along Watling Street. They could enjoy a variation of landscape. And there would be many stories to tell on their return.

They set off puzzled by Aethelred's message and disappointed that he had not written a letter in return. If writing was difficult for him he could have asked his scribe to write a message. But they knew what he had said and they would relay this to Aelfflaed and Osryth. It was not the best way to give cheer to his wife, they reflected. Perhaps the rumours about a quarrel were correct.

It was by now beautiful autumn weather. The leaves had nearly all dropped from the trees and the sound of the horses' hooves were muffled by the piles of leaves that they rode over. They made good progress. The morning was chilly and misty; slants of sunshine gradually penetrated the mist and brightened the landscape. Before evening had fallen they had reached the crossroads between Watling Street and Ryknild Street. They decided to set up their shelter there and camp there for the night. They found a secluded spot not far from the track on a slight incline.

'Let's make a campfire,' Osbert said to his companions. 'We can heat some water and have a hot drink and it will keep us warm.' They looked around for sticks to pile together. Luckily the twigs were dry and they found their tinderbox with its flint and steel tools to light the campfire. 'If we want to keep the fire alight why do we not cut up those two wooden stakes?' said the youngest monk. 'It seems odd that they have just been driven into the ground there. They could be cut up with our knives and the fire may last a bit longer.'

'That is a good idea,' said Osbert. 'I can't understand why those two stakes are there. Perhaps someone was thinking of building their house here and decided that it was too isolated a spot.'

So the monks collected their firewood and before long the campfire was ablaze. They sat around it warming their hands. They ate their bread and cheese and drank some ale. They felt relaxed. They sang songs such as troubadours sing. 'We will be scaring any wolves away,' said the youngest monk with a grin. 'That is no bad thing.' They knew that they would remember this camaraderie for a long time. They then strung up a small shelter suspended under the trees and put their bedding rolls under it. All of them slept a sound sleep, tired from their long trek from Tamworth.

When they woke in the morning it was daylight. Again the sunlight was streaking down in narrow shafts between the trees.

'What is that?' called Osbert. 'Something is glittering in the trees. How strange. Maybe that magpie has picked up a bauble from somewhere.' And they could see a sleek magpie looking down upon them with apparent disdain.

They looked closer. The youngest monk, who was only eighteen years old, climbed the first few branches of the tree, snagging his robes as he did so. He took hold of the sparkling item and handed it down to his companions, who gasped in astonishment. This was the most beautiful amber necklace. 'Does this not look familiar to you?' said Osbert. 'Where have we seen this before?' They all thought for a while and then Osbert added, 'Have we not seen our lady Eanfled wearing this beautiful necklace? I wonder whether one of those Mercian thegns stole it from her when she attended for the wedding in Tamworth and hid it here. It is an unusual design and I cannot believe that there is more than one of these necklaces. We surely could not be criticised if we return the necklace to her.'

They gathered the necklace up with their belongings and went on their way. As they departed the magpie flew round and was joined by another. 'One for sorrow, two for joy,' murmured Osbert, 'Let us hope that some joy can come to the royal family at Whitby. Recently it seems to have been only sadness that has befallen that family.'

A few days later they reached Whitby. They passed on the various messages from Aethelred hoping that Eanfled and her daughters would not be too disappointed. Instead of that, to their surprise, the three women displayed an air of relief. They would enjoy the wedding of young Edric and Anna without worrying about any hostile faces. Osryth had more colour in her cheeks and seemed generally brighter. However, all three women went pale when the amber necklace was handed over. There was no discussion between them, just a general look of consternation. Eanfled asked him where he had found it and whether he could describe the actual location. He described the gentle incline near the crossroads of Ryknild Street and Watling Street and then mentioned the two stakes on the ground that they had pulled out to keep the fire warm. All three women looked aghast. Was this caused by the shock that someone might have stolen the necklace from Eanfled? the monks wondered.

The abbey was soon full of activity. A long dress of woollen cloth was being made for Anna. This would keep her warm in the biting sea breezes of mid-November. Dried flowers were being arranged in huge pottery vases. The pigs were fed with windfall apples and with corn. They would provide plenty of meat for the wedding feast. A dozen chickens would also be served. They were being fattened up for the same purpose. Roast parsnips and leeks would accompany them. The beehives had provided abundant honey for the dessert. Anna's father was a popular ceorl. He was a practical man who was a good farmer. The wedding would be very well attended not only by Anna's family and the abbey residents but also by many others from the local community. Hilda was determined to attend this wedding. 'I could not travel to Tamworth,' she said, 'but I am pleased there is another happy occasion that I can enjoy before my health gives up entirely.'

And before long the day of the November wedding dawned. A sea mist covered the shore and the headland. The weather was chilly and damp. Despite the winter greyness the wedding went off without flaw. And just before the ceremony the clouds briefly parted and a watery sun sent out shafts of light.

No trouble had been spared. Anna looked sparkling in her warm colourful robes. Dried flowers were twisted in her dark hair, which had been coiled up at the top of her head. Edric looked with gratitude at his new family and they all looked delighted. The music and singing at the service resounded around the rafters of the chapel. A large number of guests had been invited and the wedding feast was set out in the refectory. Hilda sat enthralled both by the ceremony and the celebration meal. Even though the couple were not related to her this certainly made up for the wedding she had missed in Tamworth. However, her joy at this happy ceremony was tinged with concern for Osryth. Since she had returned to Whitby she had looked sad and her face seemed to have lost its youthful appearance. She still looked beautiful but definitely now more careworn. Hilda wondered what problems Osryth had encountered. Hopefully her troubles would blow over and she would rejoin her husband and resume married life. It could not be easy for a union between two people with such a chequered family history. Hilda reflected that sometimes it was easier being single.

PART 4
WINTER

CHAPTER 10
TWO LIVES APART

'Then it was like old times in the echoing hall,
proud talk and the people happy,
loud and excited'... **Lines 642-644 Beowulf**

December had arrived. There was an uneasy calm before the blizzards. Firewood had been piled up in the outhouses of the abbey. The blazing fire in the centre of the refectory stayed alight. Frost tinged the clear air.

Osryth had heard that her husband was planning to depart for Kent. She did not want to go back to the royal hall at Tamworth. 'What is the point of returning to a half-empty hall surrounded by the hostile faces of virtual strangers?' she said to her sister Aelfflaed.

'You are very welcome to stay here of course until you feel comfortable returning,' came the reply.

The very thought of returning troubled Osryth. She was content here in Whitby. For the first time for a long time she felt part of a proper family. Her mother and sister were with her here and despite Hilda's ill health it was clear that she very much appreciated the company of all three relatives. And Anna and Edric were like a brother and sister to her. The camaraderie from weeks of travelling together had not evaporated. Quite the contrary. The thought of their wedding pleased her. At least something good had come from her own marriage. They would not have met had she not been in Mercia in the summer. The surroundings of Whitby made her feel much more comfortable than her former home in Bamburgh which had felt empty after the death of her father and the departure of her mother shortly afterwards. She had missed both her parents very much. Her brothers could not fill the yawning gap. Her world had seemed empty. And the warm comfortable atmosphere of Whitby seemed a world away from the cold hall in Tamworth.

The monks from Bardney had decided to stay on in Whitby for Christmas. No one had the slightest objection, quite the reverse. They were genial companions. It was not the weather for travelling. The journey to Bardney would be difficult in the winter weather. The monks felt welcome in this community and would return back to Bardney in early spring.

Osryth had plenty of time to think about her marriage. She confided in her sister, 'I wish I knew what to do. I felt quite intimidated by Aethelred at our last meeting. He looked so angry. All I wanted to do was to leave as soon as possible. And yet you would not believe how happy we were in Bardney. I cannot quite believe it myself. I cannot bring myself to return to Tamworth.'

Aelfflaed reassured her, 'Do you think you perhaps overreacted? Perhaps Aethelred was just taken aback when he realised that the treasure was no longer where he thought it was. Would it not be a good idea to explain exactly what we did with it? Otherwise it is not surprising if he wonders what on earth has happened to it. After all it cannot be that far from his royal hall. It must be only ten miles or so, at the most. I am sure that he could send some of his men to search for it. If you recall we left some markers as to where it was.'

Osryth replied to her, 'I do not know that he would be much happier if he knew that we intended to take the treasure to Bardney. And there is no guarantee that the treasure will be found again. Those markers may no longer be there. What on earth was I thinking when we buried that heavy linen bag?'

Then she sat quietly, lost in thought. She was worried about Aethelred leading his men to attack Kent, and how helpless she was to prevent it. Was this the usual role of a royal wife? Did they wave their husbands off to war, regardless of the merits of the war? Did they wait patiently and not ask any questions? Was it better not to know what was going on? She wished that she had thought more about this before her marriage. But did anyone ever look into the future and predict it correctly? And would they have taken a different course if they could? Perhaps it would have been better if she herself had not been so certain that she had been right in accepting Aethelred's proposal of marriage. 'Well, they say love is blind don't they? It certainly blinded me from reality,' she said sadly to her sister, 'I should have realised the trouble I was inheriting.' She envied Aelfflaed her quiet certainty and confidence, helped no doubt by her faith. Osryth was not sure of the answer to any of the questions she posed, nor how to rescue what seemed like a failing relationship.

In the days preceding Christmas only simple meals were served in the refectory of the abbey at Whitby. Different soups and bread and cheese were placed on the great trestle tables. Everyone looked forward to the festivities on Christmas day when there would be an abundance of meat and different delicacies. Flour was being milled and bread was baked. Puddings were being boiled in the great vats above the fire. More ale was being brewed. The kitchens were very busy. Apples were being retrieved from the storehouse and boiled to a stew.

Osryth and Aelfflaed went out to collect holly and ivy from the fields further inland. It could be used to decorate the vast hall and chapel. The fresh, crisp winter air suited Osryth and she was determined to enjoy this time with her family. She was pleased to have been reunited with her sister after missing her company for so many years. The two women went out into the chilly winter air, their cloaks enveloping them and sometimes catching on the brambles in the hedge. The ivy and holly and, where they were able to find it, mistletoe were piled up together in the straw baskets that they carried. Their pet dog trailed behind them, now inseparable from Osryth. When their mother Eanfled looked out of the casement window she smiled as she saw them walking heavily laden with foliage across the fields. She was delighted to have both her daughters with her. It was something she had longed for in years gone by. She had not had much say in the upbringing of her children. She often regretted that Aelfflaed had been taken away from a young age and that not long afterwards her son Ecgfrith had been given to Penda's wife in effect as a hostage. Osryth and her youngest brother Aelfwine were the only two of her four children that she had been able to look after without interruption when they were young. And it had been difficult to leave Osryth behind when she left for Whitby to join her younger daughter. Osryth, even as a teenager, was not a likely candidate for monastery life. Even then she had had a free, adventurous spirit and it was difficult to see how she would have reacted to the strict routine of a religious community. It had seemed better at that time to leave her to be a companion to her two brothers in Bamburgh. That had been a difficult wrench. She had often thought about her elder daughter and wondered whether she had made the right decision. Seeing her daughters together seemed too good to be true.

At the same time Eanfled was concerned about Aethelred travelling to Kent. She was suspicious about his motives. What did he want there? Why was he intent on causing trouble? Why was her son-in-law travelling to the kingdom of her cousin Hlothhere? Eanfled herself had been brought up in Kent and had retreated there later when her father had been defeated in a battle. Her mother had founded the convent in Lyminge. The thought of the Mercian army travelling to Rochester felt like a personal attack. Did Aethelred not have any respect for his wife's mother? If only she could turn back the hands of time, she reflected, she would never have agreed that he could marry her daughter. She knew her husband Oswy had not always been blameless when it came to disputes; many years ago he had been responsible for the murder of the Deiran King Oswine who had been a popular and well-regarded king. She had been shocked and made sure he carried out reparation. But Penda was in a completely different category. He had reigned for many years and had been responsible for the deaths of so many, including kings and princes. It seemed as though he had no qualms and would do anything to preserve his kingdom. Why had she allowed her daughter to form an alliance with someone from that stock? she wondered. She should have known that no good would come of it.

Eanfled did not want her concern for her former homeland to overshadow the Christmas festivities at Whitby. 'We will have the best Christmas ever,' she declared to her daughters. She was determined that all the Christmas celebrations would take place as usual. She wanted to ensure that the candlelit midnight service in the abbey would be the highlight of the festive season and it would be followed by the celebrations next day. The tables groaned with the weight of the meat and vegetables, and later the boiled Christmas pudding and white sauce completed the feast. This would be a day to remember. And the twelve days following Christmas would also be kept special.

In the meantime Osryth often thought of her husband Aethelred and wondered whether he missed her. Perhaps he found it easier without her being there with him. She did not like to mention his name too often but often the memory of the good times they had had flooded into her mind. Then she would remember his dark mood at their last meeting and she was afraid for their future together. She was grateful for her refuge at Whitby and her family surrounding her.

In his turn, back in the hall at Tamworth, Aethelred often dreamt of his beautiful young wife, but often such dreams were troubled. He missed Osryth but had very mixed feelings; he did not altogether trust her or her family. Too much history had played out and he was reminded of the problems in the past between the two families. The loss of the treasure and Osryth's evasive explanation about what had happened to it made him suspicious. Surely she should have realised that treasure of that value would have given her financial independence if he became incapacitated or died. It would help support any children they might have. Nevertheless he hoped that one day they could be reconciled. He wished they could both start afresh and things may be different. He found it difficult to see a trouble-free future together. He was aware that his noblemen were suspicious of Osryth and her family. Many of them had been involved in the wars against Northumbria. He had hoped that his marriage would improve relations between the two kingdoms. However, he was aware that it had certainly been a strange start to married life. If only he and Osryth could always have the freedom they had enjoyed in Bardney, he reflected. And the birth of a child would have given everyone a new focus. But it seemed as though this was not to be in the near future. He hoped that one day they could be together again and that they would have at least one child. What if either of them were unable to have children? They both came from large families and it would seem so unfair if they had no children at all. And even then there was no guarantee that if a child was born that it would survive. So many infants died young. These were difficult times. To banish these troubling thoughts from his mind Aethelred made a conscious decision to attend to pressing affairs of state and carry on with his plan to raid Kent.

CHAPTER 11
A RAID INTO KENT

'At times the war-band broke into a gallop,
letting their chestnut horses race
wherever they found the going good
on those well-known tracks...' **Lines 863-866** *Beowulf*

Aethelred was in determined mood. He was conscious of the threat to his kingdom from the increasing power of Kent. Not only was Kent beginning to be the greatest influence in London but also their king, Hlothere, was threatening to encroach on Surrey. Aethelred was convinced that Kent needed to be brought to heel. He was concerned about the fate of the two young princes in Kent whom it was rumoured had been murdered by the brother of Hlothere a short while back. One of them had the same name as him, Aethelred. This really brought it home to him.

Putta, the Bishop of Rochester, had said recently to Aethelred, 'There are great riches stored in the minster there and surrounding churches.' Surely, Aethelred thought, Kent did not need both Canterbury and Rochester to be so pre-eminent. Why should they be the foremost influence on not only the church but also all the surrounding kingdoms? And why should they be so well gifted with treasures? Putta was primarily a theologian with a love of music and ceremony. He often spoke of the valuable gold and lavish vestments and wondered how in keeping they were with the Christian faith. He was not particularly attached to either Rochester or to Kent.

Putta had met Aethelred and Osryth previously, shortly after their marriage ceremony in Tamworth. And Putta had noticed one odd thing. Aethelred had told him of his intention to give more land to his sister. He was going to create a charter regarding the minster in Peterborough. The minster had been founded a decade earlier by Paeda, Aethelred's elder brother, shortly before his untimely death. Aethelred's sister, Cyneberga, was now the abbess there. It seemed strange that Aethelred mentioned this so soon after his marriage, thought Putta. He wondered whether the charter was drawn up by Aethelred as a warning to his new wife and her Northumbrian relatives. Aethelred was making it clear that his own siblings and the churches to which they were attached would be the principal beneficiaries of his land. He told Putta that he would send an emissary to the Pope asking for his approval for this. Did this plan make Osryth feel insecure in her marriage? Putta wondered. At the very least she may feel that Aethelred was making clear where his priorities lay. However, Osryth herself was included in the conversation and seemed content to hear about it so perhaps there was no problem there, Putta reflected.

'You must do as you think fit,' he said to Aethelred.
'I expect that you have made sure that your wife will be
well catered for if anything should happen to you.'

Aethelred replied that she would indeed be well
looked after; his morning gift to her had been more
than generous. Putta still got the sense that not all was
as it should be. Both the young couple seemed to have
secrets they did not wish to disclose. However, he got on
well with them and they had many long and interesting
conversations about the church and its influence.

Aethelred missed the company of his wife after she
left for Whitby. He knew that his plans may well be
thwarted or at the very least discouraged if she was
aware of what he was planning as regards Kent. It
was ironic, he thought, that he had discussed this very
subject with Putta. At that time when he spoke of the
subject shortly after the wedding he had thought that
the morning gift would be safe for many years. Now he
was determined to bring back sufficient treasure from
Kent so that he would not notice or miss the loss of his
wedding gift to Osryth. He knew that when he gave
the gift it had then became her property. Aethelred had
convinced himself that if the treasure he had given to
his wife was not at Whitby it must be in Northumbria
in the hands of Osryth's brother Ecgfrith. He could not
imagine how it had got that far across the country but
Osryth had travelled so widely that anything seemed
possible. He wondered whether Ecgfrith had stolen it

before returning to Bamburgh. He did not trust any of the family, however warm and welcoming they may have appeared before and at his wedding. He wondered whether to confide in Putta now that he had visited for a second time but decided against it. Discretion and loyalty were not the most evident qualities in the elderly cleric. Aethelred found it difficult not knowing who to ask for advice. He thought of his sister Cyneberga; she usually gave good counsel but he was reluctant to speak to her about Osryth. His sister would be really taken aback that her brother's marriage was in trouble. The marriage ceremony only seven months previously had been such a happy occasion.

Every time Aethelred thought of the treasure his brow furrowed and his mood darkened. Osryth had seemed unusually evasive at their recent meeting and he wondered what she was hiding from him. He did not want to be taken for a fool.

The celebrations in the royal hall in Tamworth at Christmas were very muted. There were no guests apart from the bishop Putta who had imparted all he knew about the churches in Rochester.

A small service was conducted by the visiting cleric in the chapel of the monastery. There was no choir and no music, just a few prayers from the resident monks. Putta himself was taken aback by the lack of choral singing and music. For all his criticisms of the church in Kent they certainly knew how to conduct services with dignity and with the beauty of music and ceremonial. There was much he could do to teach these rather uncouth people, he thought to himself as he heard the garbled and scanty prayers in what was meant to be a Christmas service. Even the monks seemed illiterate. When he gave his Christmas address some looked surprised that someone was willing to share theological reflections with them; others appeared to have drifted off to sleep. He was not sure whether he looked forward to sharing his love of music with them at a later date. It would certainly be a challenge.

The meal at midday was simple, pieces of chicken stewed with barley and herbs followed by a plum pudding. The hall was spartan in its simplicity. There were no decorations and no minstrels. The food was limited. The kitchen staff had packed up much of the existing food supplies as the men were ready to set out on their sortie. The soldiers were getting ready for their long journey to Kent. They had said goodbye to the families. Each hoped that they would return and that the mission was successful with no injuries or loss of life. They were pleased that the weather was mild. No snow to contend with and not yet the discomfort of damp cold rain. At least they would have a straightforward journey along Watling Street. This would take them directly on the old Roman road through St Albans on their way to Rochester.

Aethelred concluded that the period immediately after Christmas would be the safest time to travel. With any luck they would avoid the snows of January and February. The twelve days after Christmas were often spent in some degree of stupor by most of his countrymen and he was determined to avoid this danger. So the ale and the excess of food was restricted in the royal hall and his troops were prepared and ready to travel on Boxing Day. Bishop Putta had been prevailed upon to stay in Mercia and was willing to lead a quiet life teaching his music and following the ways of St Benedict.

'I would love to stay here and you may be surprised on your return – I may form a choir from those who are too young or too old to travel with you,' he said with no real conviction in his voice. He was not convinced that this was the best location to find musical accomplishment. But it certainly was a blank canvas and he knew that music was a universal language that could blossom even in the most unlikely places. Despite being an elderly cleric his main love was still sacred music and ceremonial; he was getting used to Mercia and he had no particular allegiance to Kent.

The troops were looking forward to this adventure. They had been warned to avoid any loss of life and to proceed with as much caution as possible. Their mission was to reduce the riches and treasures in the churches and monasteries in the Rochester area of Kent. They were to bring them back to Mercia with as little fuss as possible. Aethelred did not want any attention drawn to his soldiers. He was aware that his actions might not gain general approval. He could see, as Osryth had pointed out to him, that raiding churches in another kingdom might not seem consistent with the faith that he professed. And yet he himself could see some justification. After all, Oswald, who was now so venerated in his wife's family and further abroad, had been known as 'Whiteblade' and did not shirk from using his sword or other warlike exploits. And Aethelred, like his father, wished to increase the size of his kingdom. A united kingdom would be something to strive for and why should Mercia, now a Christian kingdom, not be the kingdom which formed the basis of that? And so he rode at the head of his army with his head held high and a vision for the future.

His army rode on without any fanfare but with a clear plan of action.

They took just a few days to reach Kent and they stayed in the hills surrounding Rochester. It was bitterly cold at night and not even the woollen blankets could stop the men shivering in their makeshift tents. No sleep could be had in such cold temperatures. 'We will die of frostbite if we do not make haste,' said one of the men. There was not much time to waste. Aethelred did not want his men to perish from the cold. In the late evening they crept along the roads, surrounded the churches, broke open the doors and took any valuable items they could find. Lanterns lit their exploits and grotesque shadows flickered over the inside of the churches.

Saddlebags were filled with silver candlestick holders and jewelled crosses and embroidered vestments. The Mercian men were amazed at the quantity of valuables on display. Wooden boxes full of gold and silver coins were found hidden under the altar of the minster. Once the troops had got their fill of the riches they made plans to return back to base.

Not all went smoothly. An unforeseen problem occurred. One of Aethelred's men had set the main church buildings alight as they retreated. This was a careless error. A lantern had been kicked over in the minster and the flickering flame spread to the pages of an illuminated manuscript and from there to some remnants of fabric nearby. The river was too far away for water to be drawn to dampen the fire down. Soon the wooden structure was ablaze and the fire spread to the nearby buildings. Aethelred was only interested in the valuables contained within the buildings and he had made this clear to his men. He was annoyed at this latest development. He could not delay or it would give time for Hlothhere's men to react. He had not wanted to draw any attention to his large number of men. To him the fires were a signal to return homeward before his soldiers got even more out of hand. Even if the fire was caused by carelessness he knew how conflict and war could brutalise men. It did not take much. It was time to return to Mercia as soon as possible before there was any retribution from the Kentish army.

It was early January. Dawn was breaking. Snow dusted the landscape and the breath steamed from the horses in the cold air. At the start of their journey homeward they made brisk progress along Watling Street. As Aethelred looked around behind him he saw plumes of smoke in the sky. He was surprised to see how quickly the fire had spread in the picturesque town of Rochester. Aethelred himself had not lost a single soldier. However, he was now concerned that there may be loss of life in Rochester, something that he had not envisaged. The wooden buildings were built very close to one another and roofed with thatch. They went up in flames like a tinderbox. He could see small figures in the distance running from their homes. It was like a scene from a nightmare. Aethelred resolved that any new buildings in Mercia would be built in stone. In his mind's eye he could see Eanfled and Osryth. They would not be impressed with the damage which resulted from his raids in Kent. He secretly hoped that they would not hear of the forays which had unexpectedly got out of hand.

On the way home, they stayed in St Albans. It was a picturesque settlement and in different circumstances Aethelred would have liked to stay there longer. He thought of his beautiful young wife. One day he would like to show her where he had stayed in St Albans. However, now was not the time to dream or to delay. It was quite possible because of the speed of the raid in Kent that Hlothere would not even realise who had caused the damage. He may well not know who to pursue. Nevertheless, it seemed safer to return to Tamworth with all due expedition. It was too far to reach in one day. They found some outbuildings near a small church in St Albans where they sheltered overnight. The horses and the men were both tired. At least now they were in their own territory of Mercia. They set out early next morning at daybreak and Aethelred set a brisk pace. He regretted the damage caused in Rochester but at the same time was pleased about the many valuables his men had taken from the churches. After all, Kent had been under the rule of Mercia in previous times. The items were rightfully theirs, it could be argued. Their acquisition would make Mercia a wealthy kingdom again and Aethelred would now have control of the treasure.

As they travelled homeward the snow started falling gently at first and then came down more persistently. He was glad that the men had their leather jerkins with them. At least they would stay relatively dry and warm. And perhaps if the snow fell thickly back in Rochester it may dampen down any remaining flames. They continued on their way briskly. The Mercian thegns approved of the decisiveness of Aethelred. This sortie had made him more popular. None of the Mercian soldiers were killed or even injured. And they enjoyed a brisk return to their own territory. They would rejoin their own families, who would hardly have had time to notice their absence. It was still early in the New Year. It was not like the sorties of years gone by when they could be away from home for months if they returned at all. And if they noticed the long absence of Osryth from Tamworth they were not going to comment on it. They all guessed that something was amiss since her last brief visit. But no one, not even Aethelred, mentioned her name.

CHAPTER 12
AN UNEXPECTED
ENCOUNTER

AD 676

'His thanes advanced in a troop to meet him,
thanking God and taking great delight
in seeing their prince back safe and sound.'
Lines 1626-1628 Beowulf

Aethelred returned back to his royal hall at Tamworth. Several of his older retainers were there and some of the young female servants. The elderly cleric, Putta, had been enjoying his stay there. He had spent his time teaching the retainers to sing and make music and he taught them the routine of the Benedictine monastery. The days had passed pleasantly.

As soon as they heard the horses' hooves and the clatter of the men, the retainers went out to greet Aethelred and his men. Aethelred was pleased with his welcome, pleased that his mission had been completed and pleased to be home safely. The snow had started to drift and in a few hours it could have been dangerously cold to be outdoors. The horses were led to the stables, which were insulated with thick layers of hay. The soldiers emptied their saddlebags in a storeroom next to the stables. They were each given a piece of silver for their trouble and sent on their way home. When they had gone Aethelred could not help marvelling at the valuable items deposited. They looked as though they were worth even more than the treasure that he had given to Osryth. The frown left his face. At last he could relax in the knowledge that Mercia would prosper.

The anger that he had previously felt towards his wife disappeared. He allowed himself to think of her. He recalled the times they had enjoyed travelling through Northumbria and their stay together in Bardney. He was aware that he must have seemed quite forbidding and maybe even frightening to her when asking about the treasure. He had not given her time to explain herself. He now realised that how important she was to him. He himself was feeling pangs of conscience not only about his marriage but also about the recent foray. Things had not turned out the way that he had hoped. The clumsy soldier who had abandoned the lantern in the cathedral had been demoted and no longer led his group of men. It had not been expected that the fire would have burned out of control and set light to the wooden buildings. There was more than one lesson to be learned, he thought ruefully. Not only to be more in control of his men but never again to build homes and churches out of wood. The Romans had the right idea, he thought to himself; their straight roads, the stone buildings, beautiful mosaics and even their central heating and drainage systems were all things he could learn more about.

The cleric Putta was not at all concerned about Kent. He had thought that the riches amassed in the church there were excessive. He was aware of the corruption of some of the wealthy clergy. He longed to live a simple life not weighed down by riches. Aethelred did not mention to him about the fire which had blazed out of control. Perhaps Putta would have been more judgmental if he had heard about this. What was the point of upsetting him unnecessarily, Aethelred reflected.

'I would happily settle in this part of the country,' said Putta to Aethelred. 'Do you know where I may be of any use in this kingdom?'

'Well,' replied Aethelred, 'I know that Hereford is in need of a bishop. The archbishop wishes to divide up this diocese. He has made it clear that he thinks Winfrith should retire. He has got someone in mind for Lichfield. Hereford is a good few miles away from here and more than a day's journey, but it is a cultured place and I think that you would like it. In the meantime, do you wish to accompany me to Bardney and visit the religious community there? They could learn much from you. And I may well take a few of the treasures from Kent to honour my wife's relative, Oswald, whose remains were taken there a few months ago. But of course we must wait for the weather to improve.'

And they looked out at the white landscape outside.

The snow was still falling. They were both pleased to be indoors. But the thought of travelling to Bardney in the not-too-distant future was a pleasant prospect for both men. Aethelred was happy at the thought of a retreat to the well-ordered monastery he remembered so well. He wished that it was still part of Mercia. He would have preferred to go back in time to be there with Osryth as things had been. Putta would, however, provide him with an excuse for revisiting the community. And perhaps the monks could advise him how best to salvage his marriage.

In the meantime, in Whitby the four monks from Bardney were pleased to shelter from the wintry storms. The snow had settled thickly on the headland. Smoke could be seen curling out of the roofs of the small habitations clustered in the settlement below. Even with the fire blazing in the centre of the refectory in the abbey the residents were glad of their warmest robes. As they hurried around their daily routine their breath could be seen clearly in the icy air. They would all be pleased to welcome in the warmer weather. Christmas was a joyful day nevertheless. All were a little weary from the midnight service on Christmas Eve, but the day itself dawned clear and bright. Faces brightened at the sight of the Christmas meal; it looked both warming and filling and the hot mead served with it would drive away any feeling of chill. The next month would be spent mainly indoors; even the sheep and the cattle were given shelter in the outhouses.

The winter was a good time to get on with the illustration of manuscripts; Osryth was eager to learn a new skill and assisted her sister Aelfflaed in her handiwork. And, as ever, Eanfled was embroidering her fabrics. Woollen hand warmers were necessary to stop her hands from getting cold and stiffening up. She showed Osryth the secrets of her craft. Osryth was keen to improve her needlework. She imagined herself at Bardney and thought how useful these new skills may prove to be.

Osryth resolved to return to Bardney in the early spring. She remembered the lime woods and looked forward to them being in leaf. The wild flowers and the insects abounded there and a few walks along the riverbank would clear her head. She would accompany her four companions from there on their return. She did not know when she could face Tamworth again and a brief respite in a place that she and Aethelred both loved might help her to decide.

The winter frosts soon lessened and the early spring bulbs emerged slowly in the damp ground. Osryth became impatient to see Bardney and its surroundings again. She was in a dilemma about the best way to travel. Travelling to York and then across the country along the old Roman road Ermine Street to Lincoln was a possibility. But it would be quicker to go by boat. Half the time. Perhaps a bit more dangerous but a more pleasant way of travelling. So, having discussed this with the monks from Bardney they decided to go by sea. Prayers were said before departure and a sturdy boat chosen. The same boatman who had taken Osryth and Aethelred the previous April would transport them. Osryth knew that he was practical and cheerful and well versed in the coastline of that part of the country. In his turn, the boatman could not help wondering why Osryth was at Whitby on her own rather than with the handsome young man she had travelled with previously. And why was she going to Bardney rather than to Tamworth? he thought. He did not want to ask awkward questions and so kept his counsel. He managed to find six strong oarsman to accompany them. Sails would be no good with an adverse wind. There would be no time for riddles on this journey.

They set out at early dawn at the beginning of March. They struggled with the winds but at least they were gentle breezes rather than gale force. The six oarsmen plied their trade. The fresh air suited Osryth and she looked forward to seeing her beloved Bardney again. Last year she had seen the vestiges of bluebells in the lime woods and beyond. This year she could see them grow anew along with the buttercups and see the many and colourful butterflies flit around. She sat there dreaming of the wide open spaces. The older travellers were more phlegmatic. The monks just looked forward to arriving at their destination safely; sailing was not one of their usual pastimes and the motion of the boat made at least one of them feel queasy. But progress was made and it did not seem an age before they were travelling down the river Witham towards Bardney. The boat was moored overnight and the next morning they set off again. Osryth had a feeling of anticipation. She could not work out why. She thought that Aethelred would be either in Kent or Tamworth. Word had not reached her about his visit to Bardney. As they approached Bardney she felt as though she were in a dream-like state. The boat glided along the river. She caught a glimpse first of the lime woodlands and then a short distance away the impressive outline of monastery buildings. She knew she would be happy to spend the rest of her life in this place. She considered this to be her destiny and she would spend all her efforts in making it a place of pilgrimage.

They each disembarked in turn, the monks moving quite stiffly after their cramped positions in the boat. Each of them took their small bag of belongings with them, pleased to have reached their destination. They invited the boatmen to accompany them and sample the monastery food; this invitation was gladly accepted. They walked along the riverbank to the abbey at Bardney. The gated entrance was open, very unlike the scene that had greeted Osryth when she had first visited there. The monks were certainly keeping their word about being more open and hospitable.

As Osryth approached through the open gateway

she gasped with surprise. A familiar figure was striding across the courtyard. It was her husband. She could not believe it. This was too good to be true. When Aethelred saw Osryth he was as surprised as her. Any awkwardness was driven away by the unexpected nature of their meeting. He was so pleased to see her and he looked too as though his dreams had just come true. He smiled warmly and the smile, absent so long, transformed his face. She looked at him uncertainly. Their last meeting had been so different.

She said slowly, 'We need to talk.'

He agreed and they went into the monastery and sat in the chapel. The window openings were small and it was very dimly lit. It was difficult to see each clearly. They sat on an old wooden bench and Osryth asked about the incursions into Kent. Aethelred said that it had been very successful and he was confident that the outcome would make Mercia more prosperous. It had enabled him to bring some treasure to Bardney to honour Oswald. He did not give further details. He very much hoped that she would not find out about the destruction of some of the town of Rochester.

He was reluctant to ask Osryth anything further about the wedding gift. He did not want to risk his marriage now he had acquired more than enough treasure for Mercia from the churches in Rochester. He contented himself with asking after her family and how the wedding of Anna and Edric had fared. He was assured that it had gone well and that the young couple were very happy.

'He is enjoying his life in Whitby so much that I fear that you may have lost a thegn,' said Osryth.

There was plenty to talk about. Aethelred was sorry to hear of Hilda's failing health. 'And did your sister manage to find the remains of your grandfather Edwin?' he asked.

She replied in the affirmative and told him how pleased her mother was to have the remains of her relatives laid to rest close to her in Whitby.

'Is that the main preoccupation of you Northumbrians?' he asked gently.

She could tell from his tone that he was smiling and when she realised that he was not being critical she smiled in return, 'Well, after this last year, you may well think so. Let us now concentrate on this beautiful place and our own marriage. All our ancestors must now be sleeping in peace and it is time we lived our lives to the full.' And as they walked out of the chapel into the bright sunshine it took some time for their eyes to focus and they stumbled slightly. Osryth held on to Aethelred for support. Those who had travelled with Osryth were pleased to see them together. Maybe the young couple could spend more of their time in Bardney.

Both knew that this new start was much more important than any treasure, lost or otherwise.

'Let us look to the future,' said Aethelred.

And Osryth smiled with relief. But the last few months had taught her caution.

'And who knows what the future will hold?' was the reply.

EPILOGUE

The future was far from trouble free.

In AD 679 Aethelred fought against Ecgfrith at the Battle of the Trent. He regained control of Lindsey, which included Lincoln and Bardney. In the battle Aelfwine, Osryth's younger brother, was killed. Because of the great upset this caused, Theodore, the Archbishop of Canterbury, intervened and Aethelred had to pay compensation.

In AD 680 the Abbess Hilda died. Aelfflaed and Eanfled became joint abbesses in Whitby.

In 684 Caedmon died. A stone cross commemorates him at the approach to the abbey.

In 685 Eanfled died and Aelfflaed became the sole abbess. She remained a good friend of Cuthbert. Aelfflaed died in 714, having been ill for some time.

Osryth and Aethelred spent much of their time at Bardney Abbey.

One son was born to Aethelred, Ceolred. It is unclear whether Osryth was his mother.

Ceolred lived until 716 having succeeded his cousin Coenred to the throne in AD 709.

Osryth lived at Bardney until her death in 697. She was murdered by Mercian nobles.

Aethelred reigned until 704 and died in 709. He spent the last five years of his life at Bardney.

Both Osryth and Aethelred were buried in Bardney.

In AD 2009 a treasure hoard was discovered along Watling Street at its junction with Ryknild Street. The treasure was said to date back to about AD 675.

HISTORICAL CONTEXT

Table giving brief history of some of the main characters

Eanfled	AD 626-685	Eanfled was the daughter of King Edwin and Ethelburga, princess of Kent. Her father was christened in York at the same time as Hilda a year after his daughter was born. Edwin was killed in battle in 633 so Eanfled and her mother, accompanied by her priest Paulinus and other relatives, retreated to Kent. Later Eanfled married Oswy and became queen of Northumbria. She lived in Bamburgh until Oswy's death in 670. She was Oswy's second wife and had four children, Ecgfrith, Osryth, Aelfflaed and Aelfwine. After her husband died she retired to the monastery in Whitby and joined her daughter Aelfflaed. On the death of Abbess Hilda in 680 she became joint abbess with Aelfflaed.
Aelfflaed	654-714	Aelfflaed was the daughter of King Oswy of Northumbria and Eanfled. Her father had promised that she would be brought up in a religious community if he won the Battle of Winwaed. He did this in 655 and Penda, his opponent, was killed. Oswy gave land for a religious community in Hartlepool and handed over Aelfflaed to Hilda there. Later, Hilda moved to Whitby where again land had been given by Oswy for a double monastery. Aelfflaed lived all the rest of her life in Whitby becoming joint abbess with her mother there on the death of Hilda in 680. She was a good friend of Cuthbert. Despite some ill health she lived until the year 714.

Osryth	Mid 650s-697	Osryth was brought up in the court of Bamburgh. Her father Oswy died in 670. Her mother then left to join her cousin Hilda and her daughter Aelfflaed in Whitby Abbey. Osryth married Aethelred, king of Mercia in AD 675. She took the last remains of Oswald from Oswestry to Bardney the same year. The couple, Osryth and Aethelred, spent much of their life in Bardney Abbey. Aethelred had a son by the name of Ceolred and it is possible that Osryth was his mother. Osryth was murdered by Mercian nobles in AD 697. The reason was unclear. She was buried in Bardney. Aethelred was buried in Bardney later when he died in 709. He had become a monk after giving up his throne a few years earlier.
Aethelred	645-709	Aethelred was the third son of King Penda of Mercia. In 675 he became king of Mercia after the death of the second of his two elder brothers. In that year he married Osryth. In the following year, 676, Aethelred and his army invaded Kent and ransacked Rochester. Aethelred and Osryth spent a lot of time at Bardney Abbey and were generous with their endowment to the religious community there. In 679 Aethelred fought against Ecgfrith, his brother-in-law, and regained the province of Lindsey. Aelfwine, Ecgfrith's younger brother, 'beloved in both kingdoms', was killed. Aethelred had to pay 'wergild'. Theodore, the archbishop who arranged for this to be done, was successful in bringing the wars between Mercia and Northumbria to an end. Aethelred was succeeded by Coenred, his nephew, when he stepped down as monarch in 704. He retired to Bardney Monastery and died and was buried there.

Oswy	612-670	As a child Oswy was exiled with his brother Oswald in Iona. Later he became king of Bernicia from 642. In 651 he arranged for Oswine, a relative and king of Deira, to be murdered; for this he had to pay wergild and he founded the monastery of Gilling. He became king of Northumbria from the year 654. His eldest son, Aldfrith, was illegitimate; his mother Fina was an Irish princess. He then had two children Alchfrid and Alhflaed with his first wife Rhieinmelth of Rheged. Eanfled was his second wife. He had four children with her. In 664 he hosted the Synod of Whitby. At one stage of his reign he handed over Ecgfrith to the royal hall in Tamworth in effect as a hostage. And later he handed over Aelfflaed after his success at the Battle of Winwaed. He died of illness in 670. He was buried at Whitby Abbey.
Oswald	604-642	Oswald was born in 604, the son of Aethelfrith and Acha. He married Kineburga. Their son was Ethelwald of Deira. At an early age Oswald was exiled on the island of Iona. He became well versed there in Celtic Christianity. He introduced Celtic missionaries to the north of England. After his elder brother Eanfrith had been killed by the Welsh king Cadwallon he became king of Northumbria. He defeated Cadwallon at the Battle of Heavenfield near Hexham. He himself was defeated by Penda in 642 and died on the battlefield at Maserfield in the area of Oswestry. His body was dismembered and his limbs were placed on stakes. His body parts were reputed to have healing qualities long after his death.

Penda	?-655	Penda was married to Cynewise. He was king of Mercia from about 633-655. He had several children. His three sons were Paeda, Wulfhere and Aethelred, all of whom in turn became kings of Mercia, and his daughters Cyneberga and Cyneswith both eventually lived in religious communities. Although he was pagan all his children became Christian, The first one to do so was Paeda, who converted in order to marry Oswy's eldest daughter. Several of his extended family became venerated as saints. He was known for his warlike exploits and he was a particular thorn in the side of Oswy when they were both kings of their respective kingdoms. Penda had defeated Edwin in battle at the Battle of Hatfield Chase near Doncaster in 633. He later vanquished Oswald in 642 at the Battle of Maserfield near Oswestry.
Hilda	614-680	Hilda was a cousin of Eanfled. She founded a monastery at Hartlepool with land donated by Oswy of Northumbria and then moved to Whitby. Again this was one of the twelve monasteries given land by Oswy. Six were in Bernicia and six in Deira, the two provinces that were separate but later made up the kingdom of Northumbria. She was present at the Synod of Whitby in 664. She was of the Celtic persuasion but managed to bridge the gap between that and the Roman ways. She was a very successful abbess; several of her monks went on to become bishops and she is credited with recognising and nurturing the talents of Caedmon, the poet.

Caedmon	657-c.680	Caedmon could not read or write but became the first English poet. It is said that he had a dream and that this gave him the courage to compose and relate his verse. His verse became well known and was written down by others. Only one poem remains in written form, the one that is quoted in this book in Chapter 1. Bede describes Caedmon in his 'Ecclesiastical History of the English People.'
Ecgfrith	645-685	King of Deira 664-670 and then king of Northumbria from 670-685. Initially unhappily married to an older lady who left him for a religious life in the Fens, he then married Eormenberg, his second wife. He disliked Wilfred, the bishop of Northumbria. He defeated Wulfhere in AD 674 and claimed the province of Lindsey, which included Lincoln and Bardney. Aethelred, who fought against him in AD 679 reclaimed the area. In 685 Ecgfrith was killed in battle when he fought against the Picts. Ecgfrith was buried on Iona and succeeded by his half-brother Aldfrith.
James the Deacon	c.600-670s	Accompanied Paulinus from Rome. He stayed near York when Paulinus went to Kent. He was connected to Lincoln.

CHRONOLOGY

NOTABLE DATES

AD

625   Paulinus was made bishop of the Northumbrians by
      the Archbishop Justus.

626   Eanfled, daughter of King Edwin, was baptised in
      June.

627   King Edwin and his council were baptised in York at
      Easter.

633   King Edwin was killed at the Battle of Hatfield
      Chase near Doncaster.

642   Oswald, king of Northumbria, was killed at
      Maserfield near Oswestry.

651   Oswine, king of Deira, was murdered at the behest
      of Oswy.

653   Paeda, son of Penda, married Ahlflaed, daughter of
      Oswy by his first wife.

655   Oswy killed Penda at the Battle of the Winwaed.

656   Paeda was killed in Northumbria, some said with
      the connivance of his wife.

670   Oswy dies of illness.

670   Eanfled joins her daughter Aelfflaed and cousin
      Hilda at Whitby.

675   Osryth marries Aethelred. Osryth travels to Bardney
      from Oswestry, translating the remains of her long

deceased uncle, King Oswald.

676   Aethelred travels to Kent. He ransacks Rochester
and lays it waste.

BACKGROUND TO THE BOOK

This book is a work of fiction. The theme was inspired by the discovery in 2009 of the Staffordshire Hoard, a large quantity of very valuable treasure that had been buried near the crossroads of Watling Street and Ryknild Street. It is said by some experts to date back to approximately AD 675. It consisted mainly of remnants of sword fittings and helmets and included at least one cross. There was some evidence that it came from at least one battle and that from the quantity of gold and jewellery it must have originated from those of high status. There was evidence of a Christian influence.

I looked back to see what was happening in Mercia and Northumbria in the year AD 675.

The year AD 675 was an eventful one for both the Northumbrian and Mercian royal families. Osryth is a particularly interesting example, a Northumbrian princess who married the youngest son of Penda, Aethelred. The latter had just become king of Mercia after the death of his elder brother Wulfhere. The history books are quite sketchy about the life of Osryth, but it must have been a strain to have a trouble-free marriage with the background of tense relations between Mercia and Northumbria. Her part in taking Oswald's body to Bardney was particularly remarkable. Travel was not easy in those days even for men, and there were many hazards including brigands and wild animals. The actual physical hurdles of travelling long distances were daunting.

POSTSCRIPT

I have deliberately used modern place names rather than the Anglo-Saxon place names. However, some readers may be curious to know about some Anglo-Saxon words relevant to this book. I have listed some below.

		Anglo-Saxon name
Morning gift	-	Morgengifu
Plight one's troth	-	Betroth
Wrapping of hands	-	Handfæstung

Place Names	**Anglo-Saxon name**	**Meaning**
Whitby	Streonshalh	'fort bay' or 'tower bay'
Hartlepool	Heruteu	'the island of the hart'
Bamburgh	Bebbanburg	'fortified town of Queen Bebba'
Bardney	Bardenai	'island of a man called Bearda'
Lindisfarne	Lindisfearena	'traveller from Lindsey'
Mercia	Mierce	'boundary people'
Tamworth	Tameworth	'fortified enclosure by the Tame'
Lichfield	Lyccidfelth	'field of the dead' or 'watered field'

The Germanic tribes who came to England in the 5th century AD left many place names after them. The Angles gave their name to East Anglia and to England itself. Sussex, Middlesex and Wessex were named after the South, Middle and West Saxons.

The English Heritage website *https://www.english-heritage.org.uk* contains a mine of information about Anglo-Saxon England and some of the locations that I have described.

It has been useful to read about wedding ceremonies in Anglo-Saxon times. Articles such as the one by Richard Denning on his 2011 website *www.richarddenning.co.uk* are very informative. Although many of the customs described date back to pagan times many of them carried on for many years. Even today there is a harking back to the old traditions.

For anyone wishing to know more about Anglo-Saxon history, the book *The Ecclesiastical History of the English People* completed by Bede in AD 731 and *The Anglo-Saxon Chronicles,* a collection of manuscripts in Old English, are both good starting points and are easier to read in translation. That also applies to the poem Beowulf written by an unknown poet, an epic poem that manages to bring this era to life. I have quoted from the version of 'Beowulf' translated by Seamus Heaney in an edition published by Faber and Faber in the year 2000. I am grateful to the latter for giving permission to use the extracts.

Before writing this book I immersed myself in the history of the period. Among my research I have delved into the book *Anglo-Saxon England-A History of England* by Peter Hunter Blair, published by The Folio Society in 1997. Many other books describing this era have been published.

I have visited many of the places I describe in this book and I have tried to imagine and re-create what they were like in Anglo-Saxon times. I have also been to the British Library exhibition of *'Anglo-Saxon Kingdoms: Art, Word, War'* in early 2019. There was a wealth of Anglo-Saxon manuscripts there and also some treasures from the Staffordshire Hoard.

This novel covers a fascinating period of history and it is hoped that this book will illuminate a particular year in the Anglo-Saxon era stretching from early 675 to the spring of AD 676.

ACKNOWLEDGEMENTS

I would like to thank my family for their encouragement, their patience and their input.

I would also like to thank my publishers for their invaluable assistance.